Perhaps it was because she was only half Greek that Clea wasn't too enthusiastic about the marriage her stepfather was arranging for her—although she wouldn't have dreamed of defying him. Until Ben Winter came along to turn all her feelings upside down. Yet wasn't Ben just manipulating her, the way her stepfather had always done?

Books you will enjoy
by CHARLOTTE LAMB

COMPULSION

Why was Lissa so reluctant to name the day of her marriage to Chris? It wasn't as if she hadn't known him long enough, and she both loved him and depended on him. What was she afraid of? Shouldn't she be far more wary of the mysterious, reckless Luc Ferrier?

STRANGER IN THE NIGHT

Ever since her terrifying and shameful encounter with Luke Murry when she was eighteen, Clare had avoided men—until she met Lacey Janson and began to lose some of her fear. Why did Luke have to turn up again at that precise moment, making Macey suspect the worst of her?

MAN'S WORLD

After the bitterness and disillusion of her marriage, Kate had no intention of ever getting involved with a man again. And her opinion of them, if it needed confirming, was confirmed when Eliot Holman got the job that should have been hers. But was that the real reason she couldn't get him out of her thoughts?

OBSESSION

Lang Hyland was undeniably attractive; he was also, equally undeniably, a womaniser—three months was the average life of one of his ladies. Nicola was his secretary and that was all she intended to be; she had no intention of being just another scalp on Lang's belt. But would she have the strength of mind to stick to her guns?

SEDUCTION

BY

CHARLOTTE LAMB

MILLS & BOON LIMITED
15–16 BROOK'S MEWS
LONDON W1A 1DR

First published 1980
Australian copyright 1981
Philippine copyright 1981

This edition 1981

© Charlotte Lamb 1981

ISBN 0 263 73450 1

Set in Linotype Baskerville 10 on 12 pt.

Made and printed in Great Britain by
Richard Clay (The Chaucer Press), Ltd., Bungay, Suffolk

CHAPTER ONE

THEY were in the middle of a heatwave, Clea kept going into the kitchen to drink glasses of iced water, but she was permanently parched, her body seemed as dry as the brown hills ringing the villa.

For days the weather had been unbroken. The burning disc of the sun seemed to stand still overhead, the air vibrating in the crowded Athens streets, people moving with heavy reluctance only when they had to, and then slowly, a sheen of perspiration on their skins.

It was late afternoon. She walked out on to the terrace and stood there, staring down into the garden. Black pools of shadow lay under the pine trees, the lawns shimmered like a desert mirage in the hot air. She could hear the murmur of the sea at a distance, a sultry invitation which had drawn her down there at dawn that morning. The villa had its own pool, but Clea preferred the space and freedom of the sea.

Suddenly she heard voices inside the villa. One she recognised at once. The other was unfamiliar; a man's voice, deep and amused, giving an impression of impatience in the way he cut his words off almost before they had escaped.

'How the hell are you supposed to sleep at night in weather like this?'

'I spent most of last night in the pool,' Melissa answered. 'It was fun floating around in the dark. The water was so cool and refreshing.'

'Lucky girl,' the man answered, laughing. 'My hotel bedroom was like an oven. Most of Athens was awake, too, and making a terrific din. I had the choice of keeping the window open and listening to them, or closing it and stifling to death.'

'You poor man! Haven't they got a pool?'

'If they have I haven't seen it,' he said, his voice louder as he came closer to the french windows opening out from the living-room.

Clea had been listening to them, her head bent. She saw a long black shadow leap across the stone terrace and looked up, her blue eyes wide and startled.

The man emerging from the house paused to stare at her in hard scrutiny. She had never seen him before, but the assertive tones of his voice had prepared her for the way he looked.

Tall, long-limbed, he had the characteristic Greek colouring. His thick black hair, sallow skin and hard-boned features were immediately striking. The grey eyes were something of a surprise, it was true; she would have expected black eyes with his colouring. But the long, arrogant nose and tough jawline were all very much in keeping with the strong modelling of his bone structure.

The clack of Melissa's wedge-heeled sandals on the stone broke the little silence which had fallen.

'Oh, hi,' she said, seeing Clea. 'You should have come down to the club. We had a great afternoon's sailing.'

'There can't have been much wind,' Clea observed, her glance shifting to the stranger and away again before it quite met his eyes.

'Not a breath of air,' Melissa agreed, laughing. 'But

who cares? We fooled around for a few hours. It was cooler out there than it is on land.'

'You're a bit late,' Clea reminded her, looking at her watch. 'It's gone half-past six.'

'I know, I know.' Melissa turned to look at the man next to her, her curly black head whipped into a dishevelled but attractive tangle. She was striking in appearance, a girl who sparkled when she talked, her black eyes almond-shaped and her skin a uniform golden brown. She was wearing a tiny white bikini top and a pair of brief, tight shorts which left her legs bare and gleaming with salt spray.

'Do you mind if I leave you for a while?' Clea watched the flirtatious teasing in her stepsister's face with wry recognition. 'Papa will be home any minute, roaring with temper if any of us aren't ready for dinner. This house ticks like a clock, and it's Papa who winds it up every day.'

'I can't wait to meet him,' the stranger murmured drily.

Melissa laughed, wrinkling her small nose at him. 'Don't be sarcastic!'

Melissa's giggle annoyed Clea. What had she been saying about her father?

'Clea, can you look after Benedict while I shower and change?' Melissa didn't even bother to introduce them. She was always whirling from place to place, in a hurry to get somewhere else, never contented where she was, always in a state of excited desire to be somewhere more interesting. She had the same attitude to people. In conversation her eyes kept moving in search of someone more attractive, a newcomer to her gilded net of looks and charm. 'Get him a drink, will you, there's a pet?' She skimmed back into the house, clacking at every step, and flung a last smile over her shoulder at Benedict before she vanished.

Helplessly, Clea stared at him, wondering who on earth he was, and what had possessed Melissa to bring him home with her without warning. She knew Kerasteri's attitude about such things. This was, as he was fond of pointing out, his house, and he expected them to ask his permission before they brought a stranger into it.

Her scrutiny was returned openly. While Melissa had been talking, the stranger had already given Clea a comprehensive examination, those light grey eyes which looked so out of place in their tanned setting flickering over her from time to time in restless curiosity.

'Did I imagine it or did Melissa say you were her sister? You are the Clea she mentioned to me?' The deep, cool voice had some sort of accent, although his Greek was fluent. A transatlantic drawl? she wondered.

'Yes,' she agreed, and saw his black brows fly upwards.

'I'd never have guessed.'

Suddenly realising what he meant, she said: 'Oh, I'm sorry, I thought Melissa would have told you. We're stepsisters, actually.'

'That explains it,' he murmured, eyeing her intently.

Clea bore no resemblance to Melissa whatever, but she was so used to her situation in the family that she had forgotten how it would strike a stranger. A slender, calm girl with smooth blonde hair and widely spaced blue eyes, she had a reflective quality which was totally at variance with the self-confident sexuality which Melissa exuded. Clea was an introvert; withdrawn, observant, thoughtful.

'I wondered how you got that beautiful blonde hair,' he said, grinning at her.

Clea instinctively withdrew from that very male smile, her lids lowering. 'My parents were English ...' she began.

'English?' The abrupt question made her lift her eyes again, startled.

'Yes, my father died when I was a baby and when I was three, my mother brought me on holiday to Greece. She met Kerasteri, they got married and we never went back to England.'

'I should have guessed,' he said with a dry note in his voice, speaking English.

'Your English is very good,' Clea said in surprise.

'It ought to be,' he drawled.

'Oh,' she said, her eyes opening wide. 'Are you ...?'

'English?' he mocked, grinning at her. 'I'm a sort of hybrid, I suppose. My father was English and I grew up there. I've lived there most of my life.' He paused and the amusement went from his face, leaving it hard and oddly cynical. 'My mother was Greek, though.'

She wondered why that should make his face tighten into a sort of anger. Did he resent his Greek blood? Had he grown up knowing he was an outsider and longing to be entirely at home with his surroundings? Clea knew the feeling. She had never quite been Greek, although she had lived here for almost all her life. Her colouring and voice had put her at a disadvantage where other children were concerned and she had grown up always feeling faintly lost.

'Let me get you a drink,' she offered, moving towards him. It was an ingrained instinct in her now, the attempt to soothe and calm an angry man by ministering to his comfort.

As she passed him their eyes met and she felt colour creep up her face. This man was not the sort who allowed the sexual difference to be forgotten. His eyes held a mocking awareness of her as a woman which he made no attempt to hide.

She had showered half an hour ago and her body still felt light and cool after the sting of the cold water. Her green dress floated around her legs as she moved, the outline of her body under it rather too visible in that bold sunlight, and she felt the man following her observing the effect, although she could no longer see his face.

'That's a charming dress,' he said, sounding amused, as though he realised very well that he was embarrassing her.

The living-room lay in shadowy coolness, the dazzling impact of the sun countered by a colour scheme which managed to mute the light. Clea went over to a cabinet and opened it, turning towards him politely. 'What can I get you?'

'Whisky will be fine, thanks,' he said, standing in the centre of the room and glancing around it. Pale green walls were matched with furniture in a vaguely Oriental style; low, clean lines which were both easy on the eye and extremely comfortable. Across one wall rippled a great golden Japanese screen, the silk painted with a metallic green dragon whose claws glinted viciously.

'That's very good,' he admired, standing in front of it, his head to one side. 'I'd have expected something very different in this room.'

'Kerasteri likes to surprise people.'

She brought him the drink and as he took it his long fingers touched her own. He looked down at her, that awareness in his eyes, and she sensed that the brush of his hand had been deliberate; half tease, half exploration, watching her to see how it was received.

She gave no sign of reaction, her face cool. 'Are you on holiday here?'

'On business. I'm staying in Athens, but it was so hot I decided to get in a few hours' sailing. The city was unbearable by noon. Everyone in Athens seems to go off for a siesta after lunch.'

'It's the only sensible thing to do,' Clea agreed. She had spent several hours that afternoon in her shuttered bedroom, hiding from the powerful heat.

'And you always do the sensible thing?' He gave her a mocking little smile, a distinctly needling note in his voice. Clea recognised it for another gambit in his constant sexual warfare. Every time he looked at her, everything he said seemed to underline that sexual awareness. It prickled under her skin, irritating her.

Changing the subject, she asked: 'You met Melissa at the club?'

He raised his glass to his mouth and swallowed some more whisky, giving her a nod, the glint in his eye making it clear that he recognised the unnecessary nature of the question and had no intention of pretending to answer when she already knew that he had.

Trust Melissa to pick up a man of this type, she thought, looking at him wryly, but then, of course, Melissa knew how to handle him. She would revel in the flirtatious challenge he threw out to every woman he met. Clea had never been adventurous in her relationships with men. She lacked her stepsister's exuberant sexual excitement. From an early age, Melissa had been very aware of her own powers of attraction.

She had matured early; Greek girls often did, their bodies blossoming into womanhood at an age when many English girls would probably still be at school. Melissa at fourteen had given out a sexual signal which men picked up on sight.

By comparison, Clea had been remote, cool, wary, careful to let Melissa have the limelight because Clea found it safer to stay in the shadows.

Her mother had died when she was sixteen, leaving her daughter in the care of Domenicos Kerasteri. His warm, excitable nature could explode into violent rage and as a child Clea had been terrified of those sudden moods of his. Melissa, of course, took them lightly, pouting if he roared at her, flirting so lightheartedly with him that Kerasteri would soon be laughing at her, amused by her feminine wiles. Melissa had a natural way with men which she had been born with, never needed to learn. She took their admiration for granted, played with them, got whatever she wanted from them and basked in the sunlight of her father's adoration. Clea could not copy her. Her own character was too different. She just watched, half amused, half wry. The serious colour of her own mind was a million miles away from Melissa's kitten-like games with the men she met. At times Clea envied her that casual enjoyment of life, but at other times she realised that Melissa did not take anything seriously and Clea would have found that too high a price to pay for the ability to be so sure of oneself.

'You don't sail?'

The question made her jump, her eyes flying to the man watching her. 'Sail? Yes, I do, Mr ...' She paused, realising she did not know his name.

'Winter,' he supplied. 'Benedict Winter.'

She smiled politely at him. 'I've sailed since I was tiny. but I prefer the club when the season is over and there aren't so many people around.'

'You don't like people?'

The dry tone made her flush. 'Of course I do, but I don't like crowds of strangers.'

'I get the strong feeling you don't like strangers, full stop,' he observed.

The implied criticism stopped her from snapping back. 'I'm sorry if I gave that impression.' It was true, that was the trouble. Clea was shy, withdrawn, unable to make immediate contact with someone she didn't know.

'You weren't giving it deliberately?' His brows were lifted in that hard slanting fashion, sardonic comment in the movement.

Her flush heightened. 'Of course not!' Melissa might find it easy to fall into lighthearted chat with a stranger, but Clea never quite knew what to say to them, especially someone like this man, a cool, self-confident flirt with an unmistakable technique towards women which left Clea both nervous and annoyed.

'Are you shy, Clea?' He asked the question softly, smiling, and she looked at him and away, her eyes skating hurriedly towards some more secure resting place. The teasing look in his eyes flustered her.

The front door crashed, footsteps sounded heavily on the marble hall floor. 'Anybody at home?' Kerasteri yelled, appearing in the door and halting as he saw a stranger in the room.

A short, stocky figure in a pale linen suit, he immediately seemed to dominate the room, the pugnacious thrust of his chin evident to Clea, the silvered black hair ruffled after his drive home.

'Papa, this is Benedict Winter,' Clea said hurriedly before he could erupt into a demand to know what this intrusion meant.

Kerasteri stiffened, his black eyes hostile. He made no attempt to offer to shake hands, inspecting Benedict Winter from under his heavy grizzled brows as though he were a strange animal brought into the house.

Putting down his glass, Benedict strolled towards him. Clea saw the grey eyes fix themselves on her stepfather's face, a commanding certainty in them. Benedict held out a hand, speaking in fluent Greek. 'How do you do? I met your daughter Melissa at the yacht club—my firm installed the electronic gadgetry a couple of years back. Andreas Stantalo is a friend of mine, he introduced your daughter and she very kindly asked me to have dinner here.'

Kerasteri put his full lips together, making the explosive little sound of surprise and understanding which could be heard everywhere in Greece. 'Ah, I see.' The hostility faded into polite acceptance. He accepted the proffered hand and shook it with vigour, clasping it between both his own, a silver link bracelet slipping down as he moved one hand. Melissa had given it to him for his birthday two years ago and her father never forgot to wear it. He was a man who adored presents, loved surprises, had a great pleasure in giving and receiving them.

'So you're a friend of Andreas, eh? He's a scoundrel, that one. I wouldn't buy a basket of figs from him if I was starving.' He laughed with enjoyment at his own joke. Andreas was someone he liked, a noisy, extrovert Greek with snapping black eyes and easy charm. The two of them often spent an evening together in Athens, touring the clubs and drinking the hot summer night away before stumbling back home to sleep the sleep of the exhausted.

'Benedict Winter?' Kerasteri murmured, his voice thoughtful. 'That's English?'

The other man nodded, smiling.

'You don't look English. You look Greek, damn it.'

'I'm half Greek,' Benedict agreed.

Kerasteri was relaxed now, his harsh watchdog bark throttled in his brown throat. 'So,' he said, smiling. 'Hot, eh? It's hotter than Hades today, worse than yesterday. We're having a heatwave, they tell us in the newspapers, as if we needed to be told. Why they call them newspapers I'll never know—they always tell you what you know already.' He eyed Ben with more approval. 'What do they call you? Ben? That's the English, shorten everything.'

His mood could swing from brooding, suspicious hostility to a warm enjoyment in a flash. He lived as though every second counted, thrusting his way through life like a train, exploding out of dark tunnels into dazzling sunshine, whistling with energy and impatience.

Clea was torn between love and fear of him. He could be the most indulgent of fathers in one mood, a terrible stranger in the next. Melissa seemed to understand this by some chemical process of the blood. Clea, of another race, another culture, found it a strain to live with his bursting vitality and moods.

He drew a handkerchief over the back of his neck,

his jacket over one arm. 'I must go and shower, change before dinner. Where's Melissa? Not ready yet? That girl! One day I'll murder her.'

Turning his great dark eyes on Clea, he asked: 'Get me a drink, there's my baby, and give Ben another one. In this weather a man needs a drink.'

Clea moved to obey and Ben watched her graceful, quiet movements with veiled attention while he listened to her stepfather talking about the yacht club.

Coming back with the glasses, Clea felt those brown fingers deliberately drawn over her own as the glass was taken. She looked up, startled, her eyes wide.

Her stepfather hadn't noticed anything. He was mopping his perspiring forehead, talking. 'So I said to him: Andreas, you liar, what makes you think I believe a word of that tall story? But you can't help smiling. One thing about Andreas—liar and cheat he may be, but he isn't a phoney.' He lifted his glass to his lips and swallowed the amber liquid in one long gulp. Clea saw Ben's brows arch upward, a faint smile touch his mouth.

'Well, I must rush,' Kerasteri announced, putting down his glass with a little click and turning away. 'Clea, look after Ben. We must have a chat later, Ben, you can tell me all about your electronics.'

Clea said, as he vanished, 'He's fascinated by electronics. He has a room full of the most up-to-date stereophonic equipment in the world. He fiddles with it for hours, adjusting it until he's convinced it's perfect.'

'And then what?' Ben asked drily. 'What does he do with it then?'

She stared. 'Plays music on it.'

What else? she thought.

'It often seems to me that the real object is the fiddling about, rather than the music,' Ben told her.

She smiled. 'Maybe.'

He watched that smile closely, his eyes speculative. 'How old are you? You look younger than Melissa.'

'That's my colouring,' she explained. 'I'm twenty-one.'

'So old,' he mocked. 'Good heavens!'

She laughed, the darkened lashes flicking back from her blue eyes and leaving them wide and startled, dominating the calm oval of her face.

She did not notice Ben move, but suddenly he was much closer, his head tilted down towards her, the angular mask of his face striking at such close quarters. The hard line of his mouth had softened in a faint smile, the lower lip indicating a certain sensuality in his make-up which those grey eyes underlined as he watched her.

He lifted one hand and a long finger trailed across her mouth, taking her by surprise so much that she didn't move back in time to avoid it.

'Very tempting,' he murmured.

Pink flared in her cheeks. She involuntarily put up her own hand to push his away and he captured it, raising it inside his own, running his lips along the tips of her fingers.

Clea felt a shiver run down her spine at the teasing little caress. 'Don't,' she muttered, tugging at her hand.

'Your hands are cold,' he said softly.

'*That's* my poor circulation,' Clea told him with a faint bite to her voice.

He laughed, looking at her with surprised amusement, his eyes narrowed and piercing as he made a reassessment of her.

They heard the hurried click of heels across the marble floor in the hall. Clea withdrew her hand without Ben making any attempt now to retain it. Moving away, she went towards the open french windows. Behind her she heard Melissa's rapid voice greet him, heard him answer with teasing lightness.

It was a shock, as always, to emerge into sunlight so strong it left the eyes blind for a moment. In another two hours the sun would suddenly be pulled out of the sky, the deep dark velvet of night taking its place, giving the wide sweep of the garden a mystery which at the moment it did not have. The gardener spent hours every morning sprinkling the lawns with water to give them that vital nourishment. On the hills beyond the villa the sun had burned the few blades of grass into withered yellow stalks and baked the earth solid until it cracked across. One could sit and watch the ants pouring in and out of the dark slits in the earth, hear the slow rustle of a snake as it withdrew from the sun.

Clea wandered down to the patio again. Ben was a flirt, she recognised; she had only known him for half an hour and she was aware of that. No wonder Melissa had picked him up and brought him home. How long would it be before Papa noticed and flung him out? Papa was very watchful when it came to men. He might have taken one of his rare fancies to the stranger, but if he realised what sort of man had invaded the villa he would soon change his mind.

Clea knew her stepfather's abrupt swings of mood. Kerasteri could turn savage in a flash if he felt his

...erests threatened. He was a man of deep, powerful
...otions which were all centred upon his home, his
...mily. Because his own personality was so overpower-
...ng he had taken to Ben Winter, recognising one of
...is own kind, Clea suspected. Her stepfather had met
the cool commanding gaze of the Englishman and been
impressed—not that he had shown it, except in his
sudden friendly warmth.

He would as suddenly change again, though, if he
caught Ben flirting with either Melissa or Clea. When
it came to protecting his own Domenicos Kerasteri
was immovable, a great black rock of temper and
fierce determination.

Lingering in the sunlight she ran her hand along
the flowered climber which tumbled down the terrace
walls. The scent of bruised petals came back to her
nostrils. From inside the house, the voices rose and
fell, laughter weaving into them.

'There she is,' Kerasteri pronounced, coming down
the steps towards her. He had showered, his black
head wet and only lightly towelled, his stocky body
now sheathed in a white suit. He put an arm around
her slender shoulders, dropping a kiss on top of her
head. Melissa and Ben joined them. 'Clea is my dove,'
Kerasteri told Ben. 'Melissa is the family peacock.' He
roared with laughter as Melissa made a wry face, in-
sulted.

'What you mean is, Clea always does exactly what
you tell her,' she threw back at her father, who made
a mocking face at her.

'I can't say the same for you!'

'Good,' said Melissa, laughing.

Kerasteri looked at Ben, who was eyeing Clea in

sidelong, narrowed curiosity. 'I like to eat out [
in the summer. It's a pleasure to linger over a meal
these surroundings.'

'You have a beautiful garden,' Ben said, turning
smile at him.

'Clea always gets eaten alive by mosquitoes,' said
Melissa with faint malice.

'Her skin attracts them,' Kerasteri agreed, running
his broad hand in a caress down Clea's smooth throat.
Ben watched expressionlessly. 'She doesn't tan easily
like you, Melissa, but look at this lovely colour now,
like pale amber.'

Clea met Ben's eyes and looked away from something
in them, her forehead wrinkling in a frown. Why was
he staring at her like that?

The maids came hurrying out to serve the meal,
and Kerasteri waved a friendly hand to Ben. 'Sit down,
sit down. Do you like Greek food?'

'Very much,' said Ben, taking a chair.

Melissa leaned towards him, the twist of her body
revealing the inviting cleft between her breasts, her
smile flirtatious. 'Tell my father about your firm, he'll
be fascinated.'

'What's this?' Kerasteri asked, lifting his head, his
dark eyes curious. Before Ben could speak he waved a
friendly but silencing hand. 'No, later, tell me later,
but first—enjoy your food!'

Clea saw Ben's brows scoop upward in silent comment, a dry amusement touching his face. Kerasteri
gave orders naturally, confidently, unaware that he was
behaving in an overbearing fashion. He was so used
to talking to them like that. It didn't occur to him
that Ben might look askance at his manner.

A maid began to serve Ben with a pale soup made

from chicken stock flavoured strongly with lemon and herbs.

'It's good,' Kerasteri urged. 'Cools the blood.'

'You think mine needs cooling?' Ben asked, smiling.

Kerasteri flung back his head, laughing. Sunlight caught on his ringed hand, sparkled and flashed. 'You're a man, of course it needs cooling, especially in this weather.'

'Greek men are all hot-blooded,' Melissa said teasingly, giving Ben a sidelong smile.

Her father looked at her with sudden disapproval. 'What would you know about it?'

Melissa's smile vanished and she bent her head over her soup plate, falling silent.

'Where are you staying, did you say?' Kerasteri asked Ben.

They talked about the hotel briefly, agreeing that it was comfortable but overcrowded at this time of year. 'Athens is hell in the season,' Kerasteri shrugged. 'Tourists everywhere. The streets are jammed with cars and you can't park anywhere.'

The maid removed their soup plates and served green peppers stuffed with rice followed by fish. Clea ate without saying anything, listening to the others with wandering attention.

After the grilled fish with salad, which Kerasteri enjoyed, he took some figs, urging Ben to try them. 'They're good, very good, we grow them ourselves. You don't know what figs are in England. I've been there, I know. English food is tasteless. What can you expect? No sun there.' He leaned back in his chair, his broad shoulders at ease. 'We'll take our coffee here. Brandy, you'll drink brandy with me, Ben?'

They drank brandy and smoked cigars, the fragrant

odour drifting through the patio, the dart of an insect occasionally passing them. Clea sipped her thick, rich coffee and stared down towards the cicada-haunted pines, hearing the faint rustle of their branches in the evening wind.

The men talked in lazy, satisfied voices, laughing. Melissa watched Ben all the time, fascinated by the turn of his black head, the shift of the long body.

It was an evening much like any other at the villa, yet Clea felt a peculiar, troubled awareness inside herself. She did not look round towards him, but she too was aware of Ben Winter, the deep cool tones of his voice becoming more and more familiar to her. Kerasteri was interrogating him without trying to hide it, questioning him about his firm, his position, his family.

Listening, Clea discovered that Ben was the managing director of an electronics firm, that he was the son of the founder of the firm, that he had a younger brother who was a painter and did not work for the family at all.

Kerasteri rumbled disgustedly: 'Why did you let him do it?'

Ben shrugged. 'He made his own decision.'

'You should have made him do as he was told,' Kerasteri roared, waving his large hand, cigar smoke fanning towards Clea. 'Family is family. I wouldn't let a son of mine walk away from his inheritance.'

Ben surveyed him, heavy lids sheathing his grey eyes. 'You have no son, I gather?'

Kerasteri's great shoulders slumped in self-pity. 'No,' he admitted, deep in his throat. 'I've no son, just two girls.' He raised himself, becoming buoyant again, throwing each of the girls a smile. 'But they'll bring me sons when they marry, and grandsons, too.' He gave Ben a secretive, sly look. 'Greek grandsons.'

Ben would have had to be stupid not to pick that up. He lifted his sardonic brow, smiling. 'You've picked out men for them, I suppose?' The question was half joking, but Kerasteri did not smile back.

'Oh, yes,' he said, 'I chose their husbands myself.'

Ben looked at him, his face empty and unreadable. He turned his head and looked down the table at Clea. She was watching him, but as he looked towards her she looked down the garden at the pines, her oval face tranquil.

CHAPTER TWO

MELISSA wandered into Clea's bedroom at around midnight, her slender figure barely covered by the brief silk nightie she was wearing. Clea was brushing her hair in front of the mirror and looked at her in surprise. 'Not in bed yet?'

'Not sleepy,' said Melissa, sprawling on the bed. She yawned. 'Too hot to sleep. When will this weather end?'

Clea kept her eyes on her own reflection. Her face had a wary look. She didn't want to talk to Melissa. She had left her stepsister talking to Ben on the terrace in a romantic moonlight which bathed their figures like the spotlight in a theatre. She had looked back at them as she went into the villa and had felt oddly on edge.

'What did you think of him?' Melissa asked, watching her.

'Who?' Clea went on brushing automatically.

'Who? Ben, of course.'

Clea shrugged without answering.

'I wish Papa would forget this crazy idea about marrying us off,' Melissa pouted. 'I don't want to marry Alexos.'

'Tell your father, not me,' Clea retorted, knowing she wouldn't do anything of the kind. Melissa might be able to twist her father round her little finger in everything else, but as far as his plans for her marriage went he was immovable, and Melissa knew it. She was only whistling in the dark, complaining in secret when in front of her father she would never try to argue. That would be to bring down Kerasteri's explosive wrath on her head.

'Do you want to marry Dimitri?'

Clea put her tweezers away in the little silver manicure case which Kerasteri had given her for her fourteenth birthday. Her own initials glittered up at her as she closed the case. Her eyes raised to survey herself in the mirror of the dressing-table.

'No,' she said in a low, quiet voice.

'Well then,' said Melissa, and Clea knew very well what was coming. During their childhood Melissa had always tried to push her to the fore when it came to some risky game which might end in Kerasteri roaring at them or even slapping them. 'Why don't you tell Papa so?'

Clea slowly shrugged. She had often thought of doing so, but she couldn't quite face the thought. She was both afraid of her stepfather's roused temper and afraid of hurting his feelings. Love and fear kept her silent and she did not know which was the most powerful.

Dimitri was pleasant enough, a man in his late thirties, wealthy, not unattractive, his manner to her always careful and chivalrous. She had nothing against him. If Kerasteri asked her: 'Why?' as he would if she brought the matter up, she would not know what to say to him, how to explain what she felt except in terms she knew he would not understand. Kerasteri was not a man to whom romantic love would mean much. He was both eminently practical and earthy. To him sex was the exciting climax of a relationship between a man and a woman, the end for which marriage had been planned, the preliminary which would result in the triumphant arrival later of a grandson for Kerasteri. Clea had heard him talking to friends, his deep Greek voice rich with amusement. 'She is a woman, you know? A woman, my friend.' He would kiss his bunched fingers, eyes sparkling, and the other men would laugh, understanding him. There was no romanticism in them. A woman was something you took to bed, got with child, shouted at when she was late with your meal. Men like Kerasteri appreciated the sort of woman who matched their vital masculinity: hot-blooded, sensual, practical. He had no comprehension of a romantic attitude to life. Under the burning Greek sun it would seem a pale shadow of what life could be. He would despise it, mock it, try to bully her out of such foolish notions.

Clea had spent months struggling with her problem and Melissa was not going to stampede her into making any decisions tonight.

'Tell him,' Melissa repeated, grasping her brown toes with her hands.

Clea looked at her clock. 'I'm tired. Do go to bed, Mel.'

'You haven't got the courage of a mouse!'

'No,' Clea agreed wearily.

'I'd tell him in your place,' Melissa flung, swinging down off the bed and eyeing her with scorn.

'Then you tell him.'

'You're the one who'll be married off first. Only a few more months. October, isn't it?'

Clea shivered. 'Yes.' The months had seemed long

enough at one time, stretching like elastic in front of her, giving her plenty of time to bring herself to the point of being frank with Kerasteri, but as each month passed and she came no nearer to having the courage to broach the subject she was beginning to feel deeply nervous.

'Only four months,' drawled Melissa with a sly satisfaction. 'You're leaving it a bit late.'

'Go to bed, Melissa,' Clea sighed.

'Why shouldn't we choose for ourselves? What year does he think this is? There's no law that can make you marry Dimitri if you refuse to, especially as you're English and of age.'

'There's no law,' Clea repeated drily. Only the law of love and fear which made her hesitate to discuss the matter with her stepfather. He had been endlessly kind to her all her life and the fact that there was no blood tie to explain his warm kindness made her gratitude and affection all the deeper. He might frighten her when he was in one of his tempers, but she loved him, and she was not going to invoke the protection of the law against a man who as she knew very well would brush such laws aside when it came to his idea of family and obligation. He had taken her not only into his house but into his heart. She was not going to talk to him about law.

'He can't make you, Clea,' Melissa stressed. 'He's not even your real father, so how can he?'

'Go to bed,' Clea sighed. Melissa had her own reason for urging her to rebel. She wanted Clea to clear a path by which she herself could later escape.

Melissa abandoned the subject, seeing she was getting nowhere, and whirled in front of the mirror, watching

herself with the absorbed satisfaction of one for whom
mirrors reflect an image they enjoy. She put her arms
back behind her curly head, linking her fingers, watching the tight, upward lift of her breasts. 'I think he
fancies me. Did you see how he watched me? He has
sexy eyes, and that voice sends shivers down my back.'

'If you've got any sense you won't see too much of
him,' Clea told her, climbing into the bed. 'Papa won't
like it.'

'Pooh,' Melissa said cheerfully, flying out of the room
without even saying goodnight.

Clea clicked off the light and lay in the warm,
scented darkness listening to the whirr of the cicadas
in the garden. Ben Winter's voice sent shivers down
her spine, too, but she would die rather than let him
know that. She had the strong suspicion that he already knew what sort of effect he had on women with
those slanting dark brows, mocking grey eyes, deep
sexy voice. In a masculine way he was as much self-
involved, self-obsessed, as Melissa. Clea felt certain
that he used his voice to attract women the way one
might use the calming stroke of a hand to make a
cat purr. He knew what he was doing when he gave
that sidelong, intimate smile, letting his glance drift
down to make it clear that he found you attractive.
Melissa might have had most of his attention that
evening, but Clea had been given enough of it now and
then to read his charming manner for what it was,
and he was no more serious about Melissa than Melissa
was about him. All the same, his attentions could prove
dangerous to her stepsister if Kerasteri noticed them.

Kerasteri had been making his point clearly when
he told Ben that both his daughters were promised in

marriage. Having made that clear, he would expect Ben to abide by the laws of hospitality which Kerasteri took very seriously. Ben was welcome at the villa so long as Kerasteri believed he was behaving properly towards the two girls. Melissa had other admirers, of course. Kerasteri was happy to know that. He would have thought there was something wrong with her if men didn't admire and desire her, but he drew an invisible but uncrossable line between looking and touching. Ben had better not try to cross it and if Melissa had any sense she would keep him firmly on the other side of that line—but Clea doubted if either of them would do anything of the kind. Ben had shown her a familiarity which had startled her. True, it had been the lightest and most teasing of caresses; the trailing of a finger across her lips, a kiss on her fingertips. But it had been made so soon after meeting him and had been accompanied by an intimate, inviting little smile. Clea imagined that Melissa had received as much, if not more. Ben might flirt as naturally as he breathed, but if he tried to go any further than words and glances, Melissa should stop him. That it was doubtful if Melissa would do anything of the kind was disturbing.

She fell asleep with difficulty and woke in the cool, shadowy dawn to listen to the gardener starting work, humming under his breath as he moved around. While it was still pleasant to walk about Clea liked to go down to the sea for a dip before breakfast. She climbed out of bed, slid into a one-piece blue swimsuit, grabbed a towel and went off through the gardens to make her way to the beach.

'*Kalimera*,' the gardener greeted her as she passed

him and she answered smilingly. He pushed his ragged straw hat back from his face. 'Another hot day today, the radio says.'

'I'm afraid so,' Clea agreed, walking on towards the gate which let her out into a stony, dusty lane. Beyond that the beach began, the wide expanse of it empty at this hour, the white-crested surf crawling up and falling back with a swishing noise. At the edge of the sand a thin belt of rough grass and tall, spiky thistles ran along the lane. A great white butterfly with purple edges to its wings hovered above the thistles, wings trembling, and Clea paused to admire it before she walked down the sand.

She swam for ten minutes, enjoying the salty spray which the wind flung into her face, her body diving with dolphin grace into the waves and surfacing again, gleaming under the sun as it climbed higher into the sky.

When she came out of the sea she halted in surprise, seeing someone sprawled beside her towel and sunglasses.

'Hello.' She padded up to him, the sand stinging on her wet feet, and knelt to pick up her towel, aware that she had flushed. 'What are you doing here?'

'I promised to take Melissa for a morning drive before the sun got too hot. We're going to have breakfast in Athens.'

Clea towelled her hair, deeply conscious of the way those deep-set grey eyes watched her. 'I don't think she's up yet.'

'Then why don't you come?' He had his hands behind his head, his long body lying at ease on the white sand, his tailored shirt open at the neck and exposing brown skin, smooth and firm over the muscled throat and the part of his shoulder left to view by the stretch of his arms.

'Me?' Clea had a peculiar desire to cover herself with the towel in her hands, knowing she was far too conscious of the drift of his eyes down from her small, high breasts to her bare legs. The morning sun gave her wet skin a polished gleam, the delicate golden tan like the silk down on a peach.

'You came for Melissa,' she said, picking up her sunglasses and swinging them in her hand. 'I'll tell her you're here. I expect she's up by now.' In fact, she was pretty sure Melissa would be fast asleep; her stepsister was not an early riser.

Ben was on his feet before she had turned away, his hand grabbing at her arm, fingers curling round her damp flesh in a grip which, without hurting, had no intention of being easily loosed.

Startled, Clea lifted her head, her darting eyes wide, and met his little smile.

'It would be very pleasant to drive through the hills,' he coaxed. 'There's a cool wind blowing up there this morning. When we get to Athens we can have coffee and rolls at a pavement café and watch the city start work. I love to watch a great city coming alive in the mornings. You really get to know it then.'

Clea looked down at her arm. The enclosing hand, darker in skin tone than her own, enforced an effortless grip on her, his fingers sinewy.

'I'll tell Melissa you're here,' she repeated.

'Why won't you come?' Ben's voice had a sharp ring, the probe of his eyes fierce. It annoyed him that she should show reluctance. She was supposed to jump at the chance to be alone with him, no doubt.

'Will you let go of my arm, please? You're hurting!'

His fingers tightened rather than slackened, the grey eyes turning darker, filling with impatience. 'No, I'm not hurting you!'

He hadn't been, it was true, but now he was, and she sensed that he was doing it deliberately, his fingers biting into her. She looked down, trying to control a strange trembling which had begun inside her, in the pit of her stomach, as though she had swallowed a butterfly which was trying to escape.

A seagull flew overhead, its shadow casting a black arrow on the sand beside them until it vanished. 'I must get back,' she said without looking at him.

'I want you to come to Athens with me,' Ben said forcefully.

'I can't,' Clea protested.

'Why not?'

'My stepfather wouldn't like it.'

There was a silence. She felt Ben's eyes fixed on her face and wondered what he was thinking. Whatever it was, he released her, almost flinging her arm away, and Clea, without waiting to say another word, fled away.

Melissa sprawled fast asleep on the bed, her black head pillowed, her arm flung up over the face. Clea paused, wondering whether to wake her or not, then bent to shake her shoulder.

'Mmm?' Melissa pulled herself away, groaning, turning her face into the pillow.

'Mel, wake up!'

'Go away, I'm asleep.'

'Ben's here,' Clea told her.

'What?' There was a faint wakening realisation in the voice, but Melissa didn't move.

'He says you promised to go for a drive to Athens for breakfast.'

Melissa flung over, both arms wide, eyes flying open. 'So I did. He's here? Oh, and I'm not ready!' She leapt out of bed, her hair tousled with sleep. 'Tell him I'll be ten minutes.'

Clea hesitated, biting her lower lip. 'Do you think you should go? Papa won't like it.'

'Then don't tell him. Go on, go on, tell Ben to wait for me in the car outside.' Melissa flapped a hand at her and rushed off to shower.

Clea went into her own room and slipped out of her swimsuit, took a quick shower and dried herself before getting dressed in a cream dress which left her arms and most of her legs bare. When she had brushed her hair into its usual smooth curve she went down into the hall. The front of the villa was built facing inland across to the purple hills. Opening the front door, Clea at once saw Ben's car on the driveway. He was leaning on it in a graceful posture, watching her as she looked towards him.

Clea walked over to him. 'Melissa won't be long. She was still asleep and she has to shower and dress.'

He opened the door of his white car as if to get into it, and Clea began to turn away. Hands fastened round her waist and she gave a muffled cry as she was swung up and round, deposited like a doll inside the car. Before she could get out again Ben was beside her in the driver's seat, the engine starting with a roar. Clea fumbled angrily at the handle as the car soared into flight, but Ben's arm shot out sideways and slapped her hands down from the handle.

'Let me out!'

'Sit still, and don't be a little idiot!'

The car was turning out of the gates, zooming into the road beyond and picking up speed. Clea looked back at the disappearing white house.

'Melissa will be furious!' she wailed.

He laughed, his amused glance making her angrier.

'I don't think it's funny!'

'So I see,' he mocked.

'Will you take me back? This is ridiculous!'

'It's ridiculous of you to make so much fuss. What's wrong with driving to Athens with me? I'm not kidnapping you. We'll have a civilised drive, a leisurely breakfast, then I'll take you home.'

Clea drew herself into a tight little corner, her eyes smouldering. 'You had no right to do this!'

'What have rights got to do with it? You wanted to come.'

'I did not!'

'Oh, yes, you did,' he mocked, his dark lashes covering his eyes yet leaving her with the distinct impression that he was watching her through them. 'You wanted to come as much as I wanted to take you.'

'If I'd wanted to come, I would have accepted,' Clea denied.

He had settled to a steady pace now that they were some distance from the villa. His hand rested idly on the wheel as he steered the car, the other lying between them on the seat.

'You're too scared of what your stepfather would say to admit it,' he told her drily.

'What do you think Melissa is going to say?'

He laughed under his breath. 'I don't give a damn.'

Poor Melissa, thought Clea. She would rush into her clothes and tear downstairs only to find the drive empty and Ben gone. Clea shuddered at the thought of what her stepsister would say to her when at last Ben saw fit to return her to the villa.

She looked sideways at him, her mouth compressed. He was driving with his eyes on the road ahead, his profile hard and abstracted now, as though he had forgotten she was there. Melissa is going to be livid, Clea thought. Why had he done it? It was the sort of impulsive, self-obsessed action one might expect from an adolescent, but hardly from a man of his age. What was he? Thirty? Thirty-one?

He liked his own way, became even more determined when he met opposition. Even so it seemed an odd way to behave, snatching her up and driving off with her on the spur of the moment. The only explanation she could come up with was that his vanity had been dented when she refused to come with him.

They turned a corner and the road was filled with goats, neckbells tinkling as they pushed and trotted along together, some of them trying to climb the hillside and being driven back by their goatherd. An old man in a loose black shirt and straw hat, he waved a roughly cut stick at the car, shouting a cheerful apology in Greek.

'Okay, we aren't in any hurry,' Ben assured him.

Chuckling, the man yelled back: 'I wouldn't be, either,' the black wickedness of his eyes in that wrinkled face supplying all the meaning of his words.

Clea fumed. Laughing, Ben rested his arm along the

seat and eyed her with so much amusement that she found it hard to retain her anger.

'He envies me,' Ben assured her. 'No doubt on a morning like this he would rather be sitting in a car with a pretty girl than driving a flock of goats out to pasture.'

'Men have got one-track minds,' she retorted.

'It's a well-worn track and most women find it just as interesting.'

Clea prickled at that remark. She could believe that there had been a lot of women who were happy to investigate Ben Winter's track.

He changed the subject abruptly. 'Your father's an anachronism, isn't he?'

'He's a very special person,' Clea defended him.

'Oh, quite a charmer, in his way, but about fifty years behind the times, even for Greece.' He watched her unsmilingly. 'You don't seriously intend to marry this guy he's picked out for you, do you?'

Not someone else trying to force a discussion of that subject? Clea thought, staring up at the blue sky. She hadn't yet seen a way of breaking it to Kerasteri that she didn't want to marry Dimitri, and the painful problem of possibly coming to an open breach with her stepfather wasn't one she wanted to discuss with a stranger.

'How well do you know him?' Ben asked.

'Who?' She looked at him in surprise.

'Your future husband,' he said drily, his mouth denting at the corners with sardonic irritation.

She flushed. 'Oh, Dimitri? Quite well.'

'Quite well?' he repeated. 'God almighty! You're ready to marry someone you only know quite well?'

He mimicked the tone of her voice as she had said the words and she locked her fingers together in her lap, the nervous shift of them engaging Ben's attention.

He stared at them. 'You're not as cool and collected as you'd like us all to think, are you?'

'I don't want to talk about it.'

'That's just the reason why you should. You can't do it, Clea.'

'You don't know anything about it!' Her eyes lifted to the dramatic folding of the hills against the burning blue sky. Although he was half Greek he obviously didn't understand the way Kerasteri looked at life. Clea understood it. She knew she was going to have trouble making her stepfather understand the way she felt.

'I know you aren't in love with this man,' Ben muttered.

'You're talking about love as it's understood in England, not in Greece,' Clea answered ruefully.

The eternal struggle of Greek life against the sun, the parched summers, the harsh violence of nature, had given the shaping force which had made the pattern of sexual balance here. Under the vines in the evenings the men danced and drank. They were alive. Survival wasn't just a word to them. A man whose throat has dried up from want of water in a stony landscape knows the meaning of water. A man whose olives and vines may be withered by the sun and the wind knows the meaning of life. All their energies went into the day-to-day struggle to survive, reducing the civilising elements to those of natural justice. It was still basically a peasant economy here, based on the land, and men like Kerasteri still saw life in terms of survival, fertility, hope.

'I'm half Greek,' Ben said angrily.

'In blood, but in education you're entirely English, aren't you?' Clea shrugged.

Ben moved abruptly, his fingers locking round her chin and pushing her head back so that he could watch the surprised, anxious flare of her eyes.

'Let me ask you a Greek question—do you want him?'

Dumbfounded, she tried to pull her head away, but was held in a remorseless grip.

'Answer me! Do you fancy the idea of going to bed with this man?'

Hot-cheeked, she muttered: 'I'm not answering a question like that. You've no right to ask it.'

'You don't want him, do you?' Ben insisted, shaking her slightly.

'You don't understand ...'

'Then explain it to me.'

'My stepfather has been very kind to me,' she began, and Ben made a rough sound of derision under his breath.

'Why shouldn't he be? You were his stepdaughter. You aren't under any obligation to marry a man you don't want just because your stepfather is insisting on it. But Melissa gave me the idea that you were very much under his thumb.'

'Nothing of the kind!'

'Melissa is a little jealous of you, isn't she?' said Ben.

Clea stared at him in astonishment. 'Melissa? Nonsense! Why should she be?'

'Her father thinks you're some sort of angel, she tells me. You were always the one who did what she was told, the dutiful daughter, the dove of the house, as he calls you.'

Clea laughed. 'I was always too scared to disobey him. Melissa isn't so frightened of him.'

'So you're a coward,' Ben mocked with a contemptuous amusement in his face.

Clea looked away. 'I suppose I am.'

'You suppose? You know you are. Or you would have told him long ago that you hate the thought of marrying Dimitri. Melissa told me all about it last night.'

'Did she tell you that she wants me to defy her father so that she can get out of her own marriage without going through a long tussle with him?'

'She didn't need to, I guessed that. Melissa is a lot more obvious than she realises.'

Clea looked at the road. The goats had climbed up the hillside, their bells ringing through the morning air, a few little stones clattering down in their wake as they felt for footholds.

'We can go now.'

Ben started the engine. The old man turned, waving his straw hat in parting greeting, and Ben lifted a hand in answer to him before the car gathered speed to vanish from his sight.

Ben shot Clea a look sideways, the sunlight striking off his taut brown skin and making his face into a barbaric mask, the high cheekbones very apparent at that angle, increasing the effect of those deep-set grey eyes.

'So what you're going to do is let Kerasteri have his own way?' he demanded.

'What makes you think you've any right to ask me that? It's none of your business.'

'An outsider sometimes sees far more of what's going

on than someone who's deeply involved in the game.'

'You may not be seeing as clearly as you think,' Clea pointed out.

'I see a girl who isn't in love with a man she's being forced to marry.'

'Kerasteri would tell you that one marriage is as good as another, one man as good as another. That's his whole attitude, don't you see? He takes life as it comes and makes it enjoyable. He treats life as though it were a chicken whose neck he meant to wring, he just grabs it and makes it do what he wants.' Clea was staring at the unrolling white road, a rueful, loving smile on her lips. 'You don't realise what a fantastic man he is.'

Ben was staring at her fixedly, his usual mocking smile absent. She could feel the probe of those eyes, but she didn't look round, watching the dance of the sun on the cleft of the hills as they approached Athens.

'You really worship him, don't you?'

Her cheeks flushed again, but she laughed. 'I think a lot of him.'

'Yet he terrifies you.'

Her blonde head swung in shock. She looked at him, blue eyes shimmering in the sunlight.

'Oh, yes, I noticed,' said Ben in a curt voice. 'I didn't need to have Melissa tell me. And as for one man being as good as another, there's just one thing wrong with that theory. It isn't true. One man isn't as good as another. Oh, maybe you could force yourself to get on with Dimitri well enough to live with him, but you would never be really alive. You would always be taking second-best, putting up with the way things were. You wouldn't be living as I understand the word.'

'You're not married, I notice,' Clea accused in a

low, shaken voice. She did not know how she had come to be forced into the position of arguing in her stepfather's favour when all her own instincts agreed with what Ben was saying. Somehow she had got into this trap, saying things she didn't really believe, defending Kerasteri against Ben's angry accusations because she would not let a stranger speak so dismissively of him.

Ben's face changed, the cynical gleam back in his eyes. 'I'm not crazy.'

'Oh, you think it's crazy to marry at all? I see. That explains it.'

'We're talking about two different things. I worked out long ago that I'm not cut out for marriage. I'm too selfish, for a start.'

'You say that very complacently,' she commented.

'I'm not complacent about it.'

'It sounds to me like an excuse,' Clea informed him.

'Nothing of the sort,' he said, his tone sharpening. 'Don't change the subject, anyway, we're talking about you.'

'But I don't want to talk about myself.'

'I can see that and I understand why. You want to avoid the subject because you know you should have spoken to your stepfather long ago and made him see how you felt about this guy Dimitri.'

Clea considered him, her face cool. 'It seems to me that someone who calmly announces that he's too selfish to marry at all has no business advising other people about marriage.'

His grin flashed at her. 'Ah, but it's always more pleasant to give advice than to receive it, haven't you discovered that yet?'

They had entered the outskirts of the city and the

roads were crowded with office traffic making a sluggish path towards the centre, horns blaring, the fumes of exhausts giving that pungent, acid flavour to the hot air.

'Where shall we eat breakfast?' Ben asked.

'Syntagma,' she suggested, and he took the crowded road towards that part of the city, parking with difficulty before they walked down into the leafy, shadowy square. The tables under the trees were crowded and it was some time before a waiter approached them and took their order.

Ben leaned back in his chair, studying her intently, making her nervously aware of the narrowed probe of his stare.

'I can't make you out,' he said. 'I don't understand what makes you tick at all.'

'How should you? We barely know each other.'

'What's that got to do with it? I knew Melissa within five minutes of meeting her.'

Clea caught the cynical twist of his mouth as he said that and felt a coldness on the back of her neck. She might understand her stepsister only too well, but it disturbed her that this man should get that expression when he talked about Melissa.

He looked up at the interlacing pattern of the leaves through which a truant wind was moving without strength, shifting them so that sunlight fell in golden showers of dust over the tables.

'Your stepsister is a type I understand very well,' he drawled with cool amusement.

'Melissa isn't a type, she's herself.'

He shafted a smiling look at her. 'I'm beginning to think you lead a dream life of your own. You don't know much about human beings at all, do you?'

Clea felt a bubble of anger in her throat. 'From the way you talk, you lump all women into one category!'

'Clever,' he mocked. 'And what's that, or haven't you worked that out yet?'

She couldn't quite bring herself to put it into words although a vague realisation had been growing on her ever since she met him.

He waited, smiling. 'Let me know when you've decided,' he taunted, the grey eyes teasing.

The waiter brought their tray of coffee, rolls, butter and two tall glasses of ice-cold water which they both drank at once, the thirst-quenching slide of it down their throats deeply necessary after that dusty drive through the hills.

Clea found she wasn't hungry. She nibbled at one roll without appetite, but Ben ate both his, spreading black cherry jam on them with relish.

The traffic edged its way along the square, passing into Ermou Street or up towards the Acropolis, a constant road of busy, angry sound. Clea glanced at her watch anxiously.

'I must get back, Mr Winter.'

He got up, the long legs uncoiling from their relaxed and casual position. Clea stood up, too, and he bent his black head to look into her eyes, an intimate amusement in his face.

'Enjoyed it, despite your noisy protests, did you?'

Her chin jutted defiantly. She wasn't going to admit anything of the sort, although she knew perfectly well that there had been a tranced quality for her about sitting here with him in the leafy coolness of Syntagma Square.

She had only known him a short time, but she already knew several things about him. One of them was that he was all too well aware of his own attraction and enjoyed the effect he could have on women. The reason he had snatched her up and driven off with her this morning was that it had annoyed him to have her refuse his invitation. His ego couldn't take that.

Melissa had made her enjoyment of his company blatantly obvious, which was what he expected. He was spoilt, used to women's flattering eagerness to be with him.

'If that's what you want to believe,' Clea said drily, shrugging.

His face took on a sudden, dark angry colour. 'You're beginning to annoy me,' he bit out furiously, walking away with a rapid, taut stride without waiting for her to catch up with him. When they got to his car he thrust her into it without a word and slammed the door on her. All the way back to the villa he didn't say a thing, both hands on the wheel, brooding irritation in the set of his shoulders, the tight bronzed mask of his face.

CHAPTER THREE

BEN dropped her at the gate of the villa in silence and she heard his engine roar as he shot away. Melissa appeared in the doorway as Clea walked towards the house. Bare-legged, her white shorts moulded to her body, she burst out: 'You thieving little cat!'

'I'm sorry, he shanghaied me,' Clea said ruefully.

'You expect me to believe that?'

'It's true, he just pulled me into the car.'

Melissa stood there, hands on her slim hips, fuming. 'And you didn't want to go, of course! What are you trying to pull?'

Clea walked past her, shrugging. 'If you won't believe me, I can't convince you.'

'I thought you fancied him last night,' Melissa accused, pursuing her and muttering crossly into her ear.

'I did not.'

'Liar! I saw you watching him, like a cat with an eye on a bird.'

'Oh, for heaven's sake, Mel!' Clea knew her colour had risen, her body grown stiff and tense. She had tried not to look at Ben last night. Where was the point? She could see he was just a flirt.

'I found him,' Melissa spat. 'He belongs to *me*.'

'That man doesn't belong to anybody or intend to,' said Clea. He had told a version of the truth when he said smugly that he was too selfish, although she had realised that he had neither meant it nor intended to be believed. He was self-involved, self-possessed. He had no idea of giving anything of himself to anyone else, and in marriage one had to do just that, give openly of oneself.

'Where have you been?' Melissa demanded, pursuing her and refusing to be shaken off.

'Athens.'

'He was taking me there!'

'He's a man who sticks to a plan,' Clea said bitterly. 'He just changed one of the characters in his little scene.'

Melissa gaped at her, round-eyed. 'You sound really mad with him.' She flung herself down on Clea's bed and asked interestedly: 'Did he make a pass?'

Clea didn't answer that. 'Why did you tell him about Dimitri? I wish you wouldn't discuss private family business with strangers.'

Melissa shrugged. 'He was interested.'

'Did you have to satisfy his curiosity?'

'He kept asking me questions. What was I supposed to do? Ignore him?'

'If you're wise, you'll do just that.'

'Well, I'm smarter than you are, clever,' Melissa snarled. 'Because if I'm going to have to marry Alexos I'm going to enjoy myself first and nobody is going to stop me.' She leapt off the bed with a swift, balletic movement and vanished, coming back to yell: 'And in future, hands off Ben, he's mine!'

'You're welcome to him,' Clea told her, but her stepsister had already disappeared again with a toss of her black head, intending to have the last word and refusing to wait for Clea to make any retort.

Clea found when she went downstairs again that Melissa had gone out. 'Athens, I think,' one of the maids told her. 'She took her car.'

Clea could work out what that meant. Melissa had gone off in search of Ben. Irritated, she discussed the menu for dinner with their cook, a woman of fifty who lived nearby with her three sons, one of whom worked in the villa gardens part-time, spending the rest of his day on the care of the olive grove surrounding the little cottage where the family lived. The other brothers worked in Athens and caught the first bus early in the morning. Clea sometimes saw them as she went down for her swim, waiting at the bus stop at the end of the sea road.

Clea had taken over the running of the house when her mother died. Melissa was in theory supposed to help her, but there wasn't enough work for both of them, as Melissa always pointed out when she felt impelled to justify her complete abdication of the role of housekeeper. There were two maids, one of whom lived in the villa, while the other came in daily from the nearby village, walking to work in the cool of the morning without haste. Clea's work was confined in making sure that everything was running smoothly in the house. Kerasteri expected it to run like a well-oiled machine, his meals always on time, his home elegant and comfortable, his comfort the chief priority in the mind of every woman under his roof. To Kerasteri, women were invented just to amuse, serve, make men happy.

Later that morning Clea took her car over to the village and did some shopping, piling her purchases into the boot before stopping to have coffee with a friend at the local taverna, the smell of seafood lingering around the premises, the dark little interior stuffy from the night before, redolent of smoke and brandy fumes and the astringent, individual tang of retsina. The short dark-skinned owner was lazily clearing up while his wife leaned on a broom and talked to Clea about the heat. 'I haven't slept for nights, not really slept. Have I, Alex?'

The owner winked at them, carrying a box of writhing octopi into the back of the taverna. Kerasteri was very partial to them served on a bed of rice and peppers, but Clea shuddered and turned her head away as she watched them carried past.

She had a quick salad lunch at the villa and afterwards worked on a blouse she was making for herself, embroidering a scarlet key pattern along the borders. Kerasteri liked to see her doing embroidery. It satisfied something in him. He saw life in such simple patterns, dividing everything into what belonged to a man and what fell into a woman's province.

Melissa's car shot up the drive at around five. Clea looked out of her bedroom window and saw her step-sister slam her car door and walk towards the house, a discontented pout to her mouth. Had she gone to Athens on a useless errand? Hadn't she found Ben? Or had she quarrelled with him?

Clea went down to the kitchen to make sure everything was going well, then went back up to her room to shower and change for dinner. She heard Melissa slamming drawers and banging wardrobe doors in her own room, grimacing to herself as she paused to listen.

Dead on time, as usual, Kerasteri arrived, giving his throttled roar as he entered the house. He expected to be greeted the moment he arrived, to have a smiling female pour his first drink of the evening. Kerasteri thrived on rituals, order, the shaped pattern of life.

Clea ran down the stairs, a full-skirted white dress floating around her tanned legs, her hair brushed and shining around her face.

Kerasteri was not alone. Clea halted as she saw Ben, who surveyed her with mocking, speculative eyes as the flush rose in her face.

Her stepfather was at the cabinet, the whisky decanter in his huge hand. 'Where have you all been hiding? Come, my little white dove, pour us our drinks —we're dying of thirst, aren't we, Ben?' It had always amused him to call her that, the mockery of it half serious, half intended to annoy Melissa, of whom it was an oblique criticism, since in their childhood it had always been Melissa who rebelled and was called a disobedient, troublesome girl. Clea had always felt reluctant to disobey, and that long history of obedience was blocking her path now when for the first time she genuinely felt she had to refuse to do as her stepfather demanded.

'I bumped into Ben in a bar,' Kerasteri explained as she added ice to the whisky in the glasses. 'He's dining with us and later he has promised to give a professional look at my stereo. There's a buzz on the tenor which worries me.'

As she handed her stepfather his glass he bent to kiss the top of her head, an indulgent smile on his dark-skinned face. Clea smiled back at him before she turned to give Ben his drink, getting a sharp, probing look from him which held an odd hostility.

Was he still angry because she had refused to admit

she had enjoyed their drive through the hills? He was a man who viewed women with a self-confident amusement, certain of his own effect on them. Clea had pricked his ego, irritating him.

Kerasteri adjusted the hang of one of the pictures, the aggressive force of his body relaxed now that he was back in the soothing atmosphere he found so necessary after a difficult day in the office. He shed his working manner as he walked in through the front door of the villa. He expected and got the full attention of everyone in the house. His world was built around him, and that was how he liked it.

'What do you think of this, Ben?' he asked, looking round.

'Very interesting,' said Ben, staring at the black-and-white watercolour of a Greek street, the great blocks of shadow lying between the closely set little houses.

Kerasteri nodded, satisfied with Ben's response. 'I bought it last year. The artist is becoming quite well known now. He's young, but he has great talent.' He swallowed his whisky and set down his glass. 'I must get ready. Clea, look after Ben, get him another drink.' He gave Ben one of his assertive, good-humoured grins. 'She's a little shy, but I like a woman to be shy when she's young. They grow up too fast these days, grow claws before they have left school.' He laughed as he walked out of the room, but Ben gave no answering laughter.

'He talks as if he owns you,' Ben said sharply.

Clea was startled by the incisive bite of his voice and looked at him with wide, disturbed eyes. 'I suppose he feels he does,' she admitted after a pause. 'Not so long ago the law would have made me his possession

just as much as this house or his car. Women have only
just emerged from a sort of serfdom here. And Kerasteri
isn't interested in moving with the times. He has a great
sense of tradition.'

Ben watched her unsmilingly. 'You see everything
from his point of view, don't you?'

'No,' she denied, stiffening at his tone.

'Yes, you do, every second word you utter comes from
him. You don't seem to have an idea in your head that
he hasn't put there. You never make a move you think
he wouldn't like.'

'If he has influenced me, is that surprising? He
brought me up.'

'He brought Melissa up, but she goes her own way
without taking too much notice of what he says.'

'Melissa's different.'

'Melissa has a mind of her own,' Ben muttered, staring at her with a frown. 'A pity you haven't.'

'You don't know me well enough to say that,' Clea
flung back, getting angry.

'I know you a lot better than you think.' His grey eyes
had a fierce impatience in them as they met hers. He
came towards her, force in the long-limbed motion of
his body.

'It irritates me to see you drifting into a marriage
you don't want. You're like some helpless, passive child,
waiting to be told what to think or do.'

'I am not!' Clea snapped, her face very flushed. 'I
don't want to discuss it with you again. You know
nothing about me or about what I think. You're just
speculating, and it's none of your business.'

'What do you know about men?' Ben demanded,
staring down at her with a harsh quality in his expres-

sion. 'The only man you seem to set eyes on is Kerasteri. He sees to that.'

Startled, she looked up at his intent face. 'Don't be absurd! I'm not some sort of nun. I lead a perfectly normal social life.'

He laughed shortly. 'According to Melissa you prefer to stay at home. You rarely go to parties and you freeze off every man who comes near you.'

Clea looked down, angry to hear what her stepsister had said. She was shy, it was true, unable to make the sort of easy small talk which was expected at parties, but she was not pleased to hear that Melissa had said so to him.

'Before you wake up to find yourself married to a man you can't love you should find out more about men,' Ben said softly, watching her. 'And a lot more about love.'

She wasn't blind to the deliberate, inviting nature of his smile, the tease of his voice. It made the hair rise on the back of her neck. Hurriedly turning away, she said: 'Can I get you another drink?'

'No,' he said explosively, his voice harsh. His hand descended on her shoulder and flung her round to face him, controlling her ruthlessly as she tried to break free.

'Leave me alone,' Clea began, and was dragged helplessly towards him, his fingers propelling her like a doll.

'If you won't listen, let me show you what I'm talking about,' he told her in a deep, husky voice.

She looked up angrily and saw the dark face for a flashing second before his mouth took possession of her own, forcing her lips apart in a rough, bruising insistence she couldn't fight. Clea tried to fall back, but his hand was behind her, keeping her where he wanted her, the intimate pressure of his body sending shivers down her back.

She made a muffled protest under his mouth, wincing at the strength of that sinewy hand as it thrust her against him. His other hand clamped the back of her head and the kiss deepened, a heat growing in the exploration of his mouth. Clea's head seemed to grow cloudy, her brain stop working. The fingers trying to thrust him away tightened on his arms. She swayed against him and heard him give a low sound of satisfaction in his throat. Her own lips were trembling, burning, returning the passion of his kiss without volition.

When he drew back her eyes were closed and her face intensely flushed, the bruised parted lips quivering.

She forced her lids up and met Ben's searching stare. 'That's what you'll miss if you marry Dimitri,' he told her thickly.

They both heard Melissa's light, quick step across the hall. Clea whirled out through the curtains into the garden, her blue eyes wide and blind, wincing from the stab of sunlight as though she had been buried in darkness for hours. She heard Melissa giving a delighted greeting to Ben, heard his deep cool voice answer with as much assurance as though nothing much had happened.

He had recovered quickly from that kiss, hidden all traces of it, but Clea knew she would take a long time to recover. It had been like an earthquake shattering her previous landscape, wiping out cherished landmarks and erecting a terrifying new horizon. Her legs were shaking under her, her skin felt cold and tight. Shock, she thought. I'm in shock. Her teeth seemed to be clamped tightly together. She tried to relax the muscles of her face, unwind from that terrible tension, but the lava of those moments in Ben's arms still flowed inside her, waves of heat runing in her veins.

She had not needed to have him show her what she would miss if she married Dimitri. She had always known; the elements of her nature too different from those which governed Melissa's reactions to be capable of accepting an arranged marriage. Although she had grown up here, some inherited intuition gave her glimpses of life as it could be with a man she loved.

That was what had been troubling her for months, the knowledge that she could not face life with a man she barely knew and for whom she felt no desire.

But how could she go to Kerasteri and stand in front of him and say that to him? He would look at her with disgust, shaking his great grizzled head, demand: 'What do you know about it? After you are married, then you can talk of desire, but until then stay innocent, the way your husband will want you.' Kerasteri was oddly puritan in his attitudes towards women. He divided them into two categories: the ones you married, and the others. He would believe that only one of the second category of women would mention such things as passion, sexual attraction, desire.

Clea would merely make him angry. He wouldn't listen. He would send her like a scolded child to her room and forbid her to mention the subject again.

Melissa knew all about sexual desire. She found it a riveting subject, giggled about it with her friends, enjoyed teasing the men she met, eluding their eager grasp but dancing in front of them like Salome, tormentingly shedding veils without any intention of removing the last one. Melissa would go quite cheerfully to her wedding, her blood informing her of the physical satisfaction she would get and give without her heart needing to be touched.

Clea stared down the smooth green lawns to where the pines thrust raggedly towards the sky. Heat danced and sparkled on stone and flowers along the patio, dazzling her eyes.

Ben had provided the final painful element to her problem, a bitter awareness of what passion could do to the body, and with it came a sick shrinking from the very idea of marrying Dimitri.

Over the dinner table Kerasteri dominated the talk, his stocky body settled firmly in his chair, his head thrust forward to emphasise a point, silently refute something Ben had said. They discussed politics, a dangerous topic with a Greek. Kerasteri made his points with a jab of his thumb, twisting it, snarling. He was a man to whom the body was an extension of the mind, his words flowed into his hands, which gestured and extended what he said. Ben watched him, smiling.

He said far less, but when he did speak Kerasteri listened with watchful, attentive interest.

Clea could see that her stepfather liked him, found him a curious but attractive addition to his circle, but there was always that faint, almost unexpressed reservation. Ben was not quite acceptable to Kerasteri's view of the world. It was not so much that he wasn't Greek as that he did not take a Greek attitude. Kerasteri found that fascinating; he questioned him, prodded his mind thoughtfully, explored Ben's thoughts and attitudes, yet in the final analysis, Ben still didn't match up to Kerasteri's idea of what a man should be, should think.

Kerasteri saw Ben as he might have seen an unknown animal in a zoo, poking him with a stick to see how he would react, admiring and amused by him, yet never accepting him as an equal.

Melissa made her own view of Ben very plain. She listened gracefully to both men, turning her head like someone at Wimbledon at each successive remark, smiling at one or the other in applause or sympathy. But her smiles for Ben were unhidden invitations, her lashes sweeping up to show her flirtatious eyes, down to hide them and keep him watching her.

Her father observed this byplay with amusement tinged with a watchfulness which trusted neither his daughter nor the other man. The maids moved around the table in their black dresses, whisking away plates with a deft gesture or serving food, smiling, their faces sallow and thin but full of life, taking in a good deal of what was said and silently reacting to it by looking at each other or frowning. If a stranger had not been present they might have interrupted, made a point of their own, undeterred by Kerasteri's great roars of rage or laughter.

He was quite capable of leaping from the table, hugging one of them like a bear, pinching a cheek and asking: 'What do you know about it, you? Back to your kitchen, woman!' He included them all in his family, scolded or coaxed them, keeping no distance between himself and anyone under his roof.

Later they all went into the living-room and Melissa

put on a record, sprawling elegantly on a low sofa, her pleated red skirt fanning out around her, an arm curved over her black head to show Ben her figure at its most enticing.

Talking to Kerasteri, Ben teased her in silence, flicking his eyes over her, flirting without taking a step nearer.

Clea pretended to yawn, a hand over her mouth. 'Will you excuse me, Papa? I'm very tired. It's so hot at night at the moment, I never seem to sleep.'

Kerasteri gave her a glance, nodded, smiling, held out a huge hand to pull her towards him for a kiss before she left and slapped her lightly on her rear as she went.

Lying in her bed with nothing but a thin sheet over her, Clea tried to sleep, but her mind refused to shut off. Images of Ben kept sparking in it. She was restless, uncomfortable, her skin hot and prickling.

The shutters were back, the moonlight streaming into the room, making it even harder to sleep. The air grew so humid that she sat up and went over to her shower cubicle. Standing under the icy spray, she turned with closed eyes, enjoying the refreshment of the water on her parched skin.

Her lips stung and burned where Ben had ruthlessly crushed them with his own. She had never been kissed like that before, her previous experiences being far more polite and exploratory. She put a wet hand to her mouth, shivering.

By the time the summer was over she would have a bitter decision to make. She knew that if she refused to go through with the marriage Kerasteri had made for her he would be violently angry. In all probability

he would give her an ultimatum: either she married
Dimitri or she would no longer be acceptable as a
member of his family. Kerasteri had given Dimitri
his word. His sense of honour, his pride, was bound
up in his view of his word. If Clea tried to break the
promise she had implicitly given to Dimitri months
ago, she would be bringing shame on Kerasteri and the
whole family.

Drying herself with a great white towel, she stood at
the window breathing in the heated night air. Far away
the sea rushed up on to the sand with a restless murmur. Clea heard it, her face troubled.

Moonlight rippled over her naked body, lending
it the dappled beauty of some white statuary. She
rubbed her damp head, her arms raised, gazing out
over the moonlit garden.

A blur caught her eye. She glanced down vaguely and
froze, so startled for a moment that she did not think
of leaping back out of sight.

On the terrace stood Ben, a smouldering cigar forgotten in his hand, his head lifted and his eyes fixed
on her, the silvery gleam of them the only sign of life
in his taut face.

Waking out of her shocked trance, Clea darted
away from the window and came to a shivering stop in
front of the dressing-table. In the wide silver mirror her
own reflection shimmered at her, the silken lines of the
smooth flesh pale and insubstantial in the moonlight.
Her breasts ached heavily, the hard nipples ringed with
the darker aura of pigmentation, heat drawing her
hands involuntarily to them as though to ease the
strange sensation which had hold of them.

She closed her eyes, trembling, aware of a fierce

excitement. What had he been thinking, feeling, standing there?

She opened her eyes on an abrupt groan and met the fixed stare of her own pupils in the mirror. Turning away from the knowledge in her eyes, she flung on a cotton nightdress and climbed back into bed, burying her head in her pillow with a deep, shaken sigh.

The incident was at the back of her head all the next day, constantly coming to the front of her mind, making her flush and stiffen, her thoughts conjuring up Ben's transfixed face as he gazed up at her.

She had a nervous suspicion he would appear again, but there was no sign of him. Melissa did one of her disappearing acts, of course, without explaining where she was going, and Clea wondered if her stepsister had gone off in her car to meet Ben in Athens. She refused to allow herself to feel any jealousy about that idea. She would not let Ben become too important to her. He was a stranger who had come into their lives and would soon depart again. That, she told herself severely was all he was—to her.

Every time she thought of the moment when she had stood there, her naked body bathed in moonlight, she could not stop her eyes closing and a deep groan coming from the very pit of her stomach.

She dreaded seeing Ben again. He would look at her with those hard, amused grey eyes and she would know that he was remembering her as he had seen her at the window. Her skin burnt at the idea.

Melissa came home just before her father, humming to herself as she ran up to her room today. There was no discontent, no pout this time. Melissa was pleased with herself, pleased with life.

Clea listened, her own nerves tense, refusing to admit to herself that she was dying to ask her stepsister if she had been with Ben.

After dinner, Kerasteri vanished to his private study to gloat over his stereo equipment. Ben had, he told them, done marvels with it. 'He really knows his way around electronic equipment. He's given mine a tone it never had. A useful man.'

When he had gone Melissa giggled. 'How perceptive of Papa—Ben's a very useful man. He fixed my car for me this afternoon. It kept coughing going up hills. He said the carburettor was choked and he cleaned it for me.'

Clea didn't answer, her eyes on her own feet. So Melissa had been with Ben. Well, she had suspected it. It wasn't exactly a shock to her. The strange, nervous feathery sensation inside her chest must be because this heat made it so impossible to sleep.

'I'm going to bed,' she said, getting up.

'He took his shirt off while he was doing the engine,' Melissa murmured dreamily. 'You should see the muscles in his arms! When I felt them they were like knotted wood.'

Clea walked to the door, ignoring her.

'I wish Alexos was that tall,' Melissa complained.

'Maybe he'll grow,' snapped Clea.

Melissa sat up, staring after her. 'Nasty! What's wrong with you?'

'I'm tired,' Clea lied. 'Goodnight.'

The following afternoon, the humid weather broke in a violent thunderstorm, the sky a threatening black above the restless sea, rain pouring from the edges of clouds in torrents. Melissa was out all day and Clea was so strangely excited by the storm, relieved by the ending of that pressing heat, that she walked down to the sea despite the horrified exclamations of the maids, letting the lances of the rain slash down on to her bare head.

She stood barefoot on the beach, watching the withdrawing clash of thunder far out over the sea, leaving an electric blue sky spreading behind it.

Her wet head was darkened by rain, her hair plastered to her skull, curling at the edges like a baby's. She breathed clean, fresh air and could have cried with pleasure.

Her dress clung to her body, outlining the slender curved shape of it as though it was transparent, but she was unaware of herself, too absorbed in the excitement of the storm to think of anything else. She didn't even hear the footsteps grating on the sand behind her until someone joined her.

Her head swung, her eyes opening wide and very blue, startled into giving a cry of shock.

'Hello,' said Ben, in that deep voice, unsmiling, then his grey eyes slid down over her and she knew what he was thinking about and her colour rushed up in a blinding, heated wave.

'Melissa isn't here,' she told him. 'I think she's gone to Athens. I've no doubt she's waiting for you at your hotel.' Embarrassment and anger made her voice shake slightly, but she managed to say the words without stammering.

'I didn't come looking for Melissa.' His eyes flicked up, darkening. 'You know that.'

'I'm begining to think you're a troublemaker, Mr Winter, a man who likes to make mischief. I'm not quarrelling with my sister over you, so go back to Athens and stay away from me!'

He thrust his hands into his pockets, staring at her intently, the grey eyes narrowed and probing. 'You puzzle me, do you know that? I go on thinking about you even when I tell myself to stop. You've got under my skin, like a little thorn, and I can't rest until I've dislodged you.'

Taken aback, Clea looked away. Was this another tease, was he mocking her again? Or was he serious?

'The more I think about you, the more I realise you're like a blind child walking under a car with no idea of what's going to hit it. You can't marry this man, Clea. Tell your stepfather, for God's sake, make him see that it's impossible.'

'I can't,' she cried on a despairing note. 'I've tried, don't you think I've tried?'

'What stops you, in hell's name?'

'It will wreck our relationship,' Clea admitted, her head bent and one bare foot tracing a circle in the sand.

'Is that so much more important than your whole damned life?' He was talking in a brusque, harsh voice. Clea didn't look at him, but she could sense the anger in him and it puzzled her. Why was he getting so steamed up over her affairs? What was it to him?

'I told you, it isn't as simple as you seem to think,' she said.

'Explain it to me, then.'

'If I refuse to go through with my marriage, Kerasteri will be so angry that he may well throw me out of his house,' Clea said with a slight break in her voice.

'In this day and age?'

'You don't understand him. He has very simple attitudes to life.'

'He's bloody selfish.'

'That isn't true! He believes he's doing his best for us, for both Melissa and me.'

'By forcing you to marry men you barely know?'

'He chose them carefully,' said Clea, a rueful smile touching her mouth. 'He spent a long time looking around for men he thought would suit our characters. Dimitri is quiet and gentle, very considerate. Kerasteri wanted someone like that for me, he said. And for Melissa he found Alexos, who's far more strong-minded, someone who won't let Melissa go too far but will indulge her whims because he finds her amusing. You see, Kerasteri didn't just pick men with money, although both of them are well off. He gave it a lot of thought.'

Ben moved restlessly, a controlled violence in the way his body shifted. 'I don't believe my ears,' he said. 'Either you're crazy or I am.'

'Don't think I like the idea.'

'Then tell him how you feel.'

'And hurt him?' Clea looked at him wryly. 'He's not a man you would probably find easy to understand. It's all a question of the angle from which you see life. Kerasteri's father had his wife chosen for him and it was a very happy marriage. Kerasteri's first wife was a girl he had had picked out for him when he was fourteen! She died of pneumonia when Melissa was a baby, but Kerasteri loved her and they were very happy together. You see, from his point of view it works.'

'All right, I can understand a man of his age and

background thinking like that, but you've had a modern upbringing, surely? You can't believe all that stuff. Don't you want to fall in love?'

A cold quiver ran over her skin. 'Have you ever been in love?' As soon as she asked the question she wished she hadn't, her whole body tightening.

'Frequently,' he said with a sidelong, wicked grin.

Anger prickled inside her. 'I get the feeling you aren't talking about love at all.'

His face held mockery as he moved closer to stare down at her. 'What do you imagine love is?' He put a finger on her cheek, the cool brush of it sending a sudden, heated excitement through her veins. Watching her, lowering his voice to a soft intimacy, he said: 'But you know that, don't you? I'm not the only one of us who has realised.'

Trying to look calmly unconcerned, Clea said warily: 'Realised what?'

'You know what I'm talking about.' He was oddly elated, his eyes flashing down at her, his mouth curling at the edges with satisfaction.

Nervously she shook her head, the swing of her blonde hair against her cheek catching his eye. He shifted his hand to it, thrusting his fingers among the strands, winnowing them slowly and watching the way they drifted against his flesh.

'Don't lie to me, Clea, even if you've been lying to yourself.' Urgency deepened his voice and Clea felt a surge of panic begin inside her. 'Ever since I saw you at that window ...'

'No!' she broke out, turning stumblingly away.

He pulled her back towards him, slamming her against his so abruptly that she fell, her face in his throat, her nostrils filling with the scent of his brown

skin. His hand gripped her back in a convulsive movement, the muscular tension of his body pressing against
her.

'You looked fantastic. You're not ashamed of that,
are you? My God, Clea, you left me breathless!'

'Don't talk about it!' she begged.

'Why not, in God's name? For a second I thought
you were a marble statue. It was the effect of the moonlight; you looked cool and remote and unreal. Then
you moved and I felt as though someone had punched
me in the stomach. You really knocked me out.'

She tried to pull away, trembling. 'Can't you see how
embarrassing it is? I don't want to talk about it.'

'You're scared,' he whispered, his voice unsteady.
'Don't be. It's what you were born for, Clea, this feeling ...'

'I just feel embarrassed,' she said angrily, struggling.

The elated excitement went out of his face and it
darkened into impatience, his brows jerking together,
his eyes staring at her with a glittering demand in
them.

'That's not true. You just won't admit how you feel.
Are you afraid of love?'

Clea threw caution to the winds, her temper hardening her voice. 'You're not talking about love, you're
talking about sex.'

'They're the same thing.'

'No,' Clea denied fiercely. 'They can come together,
but they aren't the same thing.'

Ben laughed shortly. 'You're theorising without having any practical experience, and that's always a mistake. It's time you had some hard evidence to show
you what it's all about.'

'I don't need ...' she began.

'That's *just* what you need,' Ben interrupted, and bent his head to find her mouth.

Clea tried not to let him get her. She fought to stay cool, retain her sanity, despite the overwhelming temptation to give in to that heated urgency. Somewhere inside her a quiet little voice was pointing out the experienced nature of his caresses, forcing her to recognise that he might be sexually excited himself but that he was deliberately trying to arouse her and using a technique acquired with other women to do it. He wasn't offering her love as she understood it. She knew what he was offering her, and she did not want it.

Ben felt her resistance, of course. His hand thrust into her hair, dragging her head back, bending her helplessly in his arms so that she had to grasp his shoulders to keep her balance. She caught the flash of his eyes before he began kissing her again. Ben was furious, she realised. He wasn't going to give up until he had wrung a response out of her.

Her zip slid down, she felt his fingers stroking her damp skin, moving up and down her back.

She began to tremble violently, her whole body dissolving with a heat she couldn't damp down with the aid of that sane little voice at the back of her head. She was splitting in two, she felt. Her mind kept up that warning note, but her body was shuddering with the response Ben wanted from her.

A muffled roar from behind them split them apart. Ben released her so suddenly she almost fell. He spun, his long body tense with the wariness of a threatened male animal.

Shaking, Clea looked across the trodden sand to where Kerasteri stood staring at them. His body was hunched, rocking on the balls of his feet like a great cat about to spring.

'Bastard!' he breathed deep in his throat. His face was a dark, angry red and his black eyes spat loathing at Ben. Slowly he swivelled them towards Clea.

She felt shrivelled and unclean under that stare. She could see herself as Kerasteri was seeing her: her hair dishevelled from Ben's fingers, her dress damply clinging to her body, half off her shoulders where Ben had opened the back of it, her lips moist from Ben's kisses.

Tears burnt at the back of her eyes. 'Papa!' she began on a pleading note, and Kerasteri strode across the space between them and caught her arm, flinging her away from him with a contemptuous gesture towards the garden.

'Get in the house! I'll deal with you later.' He drew a ragged hoarse breath. 'Do you know what you look like?' The words choked off thickly and he turned away from her as though he couldn't bear to look at her.

Clea stumbled, sobbing, away from them, hardly knowing where she was going or what she was doing.

CHAPTER FOUR

SHE ran up to her bedroom, passing one of the maids, who stared at her in puzzled anxiety but said nothing. Clea locked her bedroom door and leaned on it, shivering. The distaste she had seen in her stepfather's eyes had left her feeling sick and full of self-disgust. Closing her eyes, she tried to stop the trembling in her body.

After a moment she tore off her clothes and went into the shower. The icy water made her body clench, brought out goose-pimples on her skin, but it did something to cleanse her mind of the melting, heated excitement she had briefly felt before Kerasteri appeared.

She shouldn't have let Ben touch her. Running her hands through her sodden hair, she bit her lip until blood seeped into her mouth.

She would never let him do that to her again. The shock of opening her eyes to find her stepfather staring at her with that contemptuous fury had wiped out of her head every emotion but sick distaste.

She pulled the towel off the rail beside the cubicle and towelled herself roughly, angrily, as if she was ridding her body of the touch of Ben's desiring hands.

When she was dressed she sat down on her bed, waiting, a nervous misery possessing her. What would Kerasteri say when he came?

The searing truth about what had happened was that Ben wasn't in the slightest in love with her. He hadn't ever pretended that he was—he had made it very clear that desire, not love, was what he was offering her.

The other night he had been flirting lightly with Melissa, amused by her teasing dark eyes, ignoring Clea because he was angry with her. That anger had been born simply and solely because she had refused to flirt with him the morning he drove her to Athens. Ben's ego couldn't take failure with women. He saw himself as irresistible. Melissa was happy to play up to that image of himself, giving him inviting little smiles, making it clear she fancied him.

Clea was too serious to play that sort of game with every man she met. She lacked the lighthearted sexual ease with which Melissa played with men. Flirtation was a game Clea had never excelled at. Her introvert nature drove her back on herself, made her reluctant to expose herself to mockery. The introvert is always selfconscious, inhibited by a fear of being laughed at, rather like someone afraid to walk on ice for fear of falling into cold water.

Melissa gaily skated across the ice, sure she wouldn't find it cracking beneath her, and, of course, her very confidence made the ice bear her safely. Melissa was the same type as Ben Winter, Clea decided bitterly. They both carried themselves with total confidence. They were both immune from the anxieties and tensions of people like herself.

The passing of the storm had left the air cooler, the sky a washed and brilliant blue. Sunshine had returned, sparkling back at her from the dressing-table mirror, flashing round the room and giving her bent blonde head a gleaming brightness. Clea watched it flood the room, struggling with her tormented thoughts, waiting for the sound of Kerasteri's heavy footsteps.

She didn't hear them, so intent was she on her own misery, and when the door rattled she jumped as if she had been shot.

'Clea!' His voice was harsh, chilly.

She stumbled to the door and unlocked it, falling back as he walked past her. She couldn't even look at him, her hands clenched at her sides. She saw his feet halt and waited for him to speak.

He didn't, for a moment, the sound of his rough breathing very loud in the quiet room.

Then he said deeply: 'I don't know what to say to you.'

The simplicity of that made her wince. It had a depth of anger behind it, a locked emotion which spoke of feelings he had forced down but which were audible in his voice.

'Melissa I could have understood. I've no illusions about Melissa. But she may go close to the edge, she wouldn't let anyone drag her over it. She puts a value on herself even though she may be a bit wild at times.' He paused, swallowing. 'But you, Clea! I hadn't expected to see you like that, letting someone who's almost a total stranger to you touch you, maul you about ...'

Clea drew a painful, sharp breath, her throat hurting with unshed tears.

'And you were letting him,' Kerasteri muttered.

She couldn't even deny that. When he appeared she had been crumbling into passionate response in Ben's arms, her earlier resistance eaten away by the heat of his mouth, the hungry stroke of his hands over her back.

'I didn't come up until I felt I could speak to you without saying something I might regret,' Kerasteri told her. 'If I'd come to you when I first got back to the villa I might have half killed you. I've never been so angry in my life!'

She knew that. She had felt his black, eruptive rage across the beach and been shrivelled by the force at it.

'You've made me ashamed of you.'

Clea winced again, bending her head lower. Her face was burning with humiliation and pain.

'You aren't an adolescent; you knew what you were doing. You're going to marry another man in a few months' time, yet you let someone you only met a few days ago touch you like that! How could you do it? How could you shame yourself and me like that?'

He waited for her to answer, she felt his eyes fixed on her, the stab of their scrutiny physically hurtful.

Swallowing on a hard lump in her throat, she dryly moved her lips and managed to whisper: 'I'm sorry, Papa.'

'Sorry?' The word leapt back at her like a knife and she mentally shrank from it, her arms wound round her body as if she felt she needed a shield between them.

'Sorry, Clea? That's a pitiful word to use to me. You say sorry when you break a plate, forget to give me a message. It's hardly adequate for a situation like this.' He paused and breathed roughly. 'How do you think I felt, seeing you out there, on a beach with a stranger, behaving like a whore?'

'No!' she whimpered in a strangled gasp.

'I don't like using that word, but what other word covers it?'

The colour had all left her face. She was white, her skin icy cold. The deep pile of the carpet held her eyes, and she stared at the soft tufts of it without really seeing them at all.

'It wasn't just that he was kissing you,' Kerasteri broke out deeply. 'I'm not a fool. I've no doubt Melissa had let men kiss her now and then; I've seen her flirting with them. But it was how he was kissing you, how he was holding you—that wasn't a little flirtation. I know what that was.' He stopped short, cutting off the sentence with a harsh sound. 'We both know, don't we, Clea? It's an ugly word, and I won't use it between us. But we both know the difference between a light kiss given between a man and a girl who have spent a few hours together—and what that bastard was wanting from you.'

She put both hands over her face, pressing her palms into her hot eyes. 'Don't, Papa! Please, don't say any more.'

'Do you think I'm enjoying this? It has got to be said. I've got to know what else has happened between you and that swine.'

'Nothing!'

'Nothing? That's got to be a lie. He wouldn't have reached that stage without something having gone before it. That wasn't the first time he had kissed you.'

'Almost,' she whispered.

Kerasteri asked curtly: 'What does that mean? Almost?'

'He kissed me once before,' Clea admitted.

Kerasteri said something harsh and deep which made

her feel sick. He had never used such words in front of her before.

'Are you in love with him?'

'No,' Clea said huskily.

'You leave me almost speechless,' he muttered. There was a silence, then he said slowly: 'I've sent him packing, kicked him out of your life. If he comes here again I've told him I'll choke the life out of him. I tell you the same, Clea. Don't see him again or I'll kill him!'

Clea nodded, still staring at the carpet.

'Do I have to tell you what sort of swine he must be to behave like that?'

She shook her head dumbly.

'How many times have you met him secretly?'

'Secretly?' She half lifted her head, flickering a nervous look towards him. 'I've never met him secretly, not once. I hadn't planned to meet him on the beach today. He just arrived.'

'He knew you were going to marry another man! He's an opportunist, a sneak thief, stealing what he comes across if he can. You aren't silly, Clea. You must know how he thinks of you. If he cared twopence for you he would never have tried to make love to you like that.'

Clea didn't need to be told that. She knew Ben had nothing to offer her but a physical desire which, when it was satisfied, would soon forget her in the search for new excitement.

'Give me your word you won't see him,' Kerasteri demanded.

Clea whispered dryly: 'Yes, Papa.'

Kerasteri stood watching her. She looked up nervously and their eyes met.

'You hurt me when I saw you in his arms,' Kerasteri muttered in a low, deep voice. 'You destroyed something. That wasn't how I saw you—you've always been so gentle, so calm. It made me sick to see you with him.'

Her whiteness went in a wave of hot colour and she looked away again, her brows knitting.

'I won't tell Dimitri,' her stepfather said after a moment. 'He would be shattered; he sees you as I did. I don't want him to see you any other way.'

Clea tried to speak but couldn't. She knew that if she said now that she did not want to marry Dimitri her stepfather would lose the last shred of self-restraint, his rage would soar to a dangerous height.

She stared at the floor, shivering.

'We won't speak of this again,' Kerasteri said slowly. He moved and she heard his footsteps sinking into the deep pile of the carpet as he walked to the door. 'I will try to forget it, and I suggest you do the same. Wipe his name from your memory.'

He opened the door, paused, and she felt him staring at her. 'I wish it had never happened,' he said, and then he went. The door closed quietly and Clea fell on to the bed, silent tears running down her face.

Kerasteri had summed Ben up accurately. Clea had already worked out what sort of man Ben was long before he made love to her on the beach. She had known while he was kissing her earlier that he would have taken anything he could get her to give him, completely undeterred by the fact that she was to marry someone else.

If her stepfather felt ashamed of her, it was nothing

compared to the shame she felt about her helpless response to Ben. That stung her pride, her sense of herself. Ben had been treating her like an object. He mocked Kerasteri's attitude to women, he talked about the Greek view of the sexes with contempt. Yet his desire was as much an insult to her as a woman as Kerasteri's wish to make her marry someone she didn't love. Neither of them were treating her as though she had any value. They were each of them trying to force her to behave the way they wanted her to behave, both trying to shape her in their own image of a woman.

Clea dried her tears with a rough hand, stifling the sobs which kept shaking her body. Sunlight danced and glittered on the windows and she stared at it, grief and misery slowly subsiding inside her.

What value did she have? What was she going to do about her situation?

For the first time in her life she felt the necessity of reaching an understanding of herself, not just as a person, but as a person within society, a human being under the pressure of resisting and withstanding the desire of other human beings to make her submit to their view of her.

She faced the prospect of doing as her stepfather wished and marrying Dimitri.

That was impossible, she admitted now. She could not go through with it, whether or not that meant the end of her life here in Greece. Until now she had been torn between the realisation that she hated the idea of marrying Dimitri and the fear of what a refusal would entail. It meant painful amputation of her family life. She would have to leave here, leave Greece.

Kerasteri would not want to see her if she refused to marry Dimitri, specially now that he had seen her with Ben. He would believe her refusal came from a very different cause.

Clea had not wanted to face that. She had been struggling with those painful ideas for months. It was like the struggle of a moth escaping from a chrysalis, a bitter wearying fight to reach the light.

She hadn't been able to clarify her tormented thoughts until now because she hadn't seen them in just this light. Only now did her mind grasp the equation.

Kerasteri and Ben had fused the problem, making it one, and totally clear. If Clea yielded to either of them she was relinquishing her value as a woman, allowing other people to manipulate her and control her like a puppet. Melissa was equipped by nature to accept life as it came, escaping from the male domination of her daily existence by craft and furtive little forays into enjoyment. Melissa would somehow manage to get the most out of life even if she had to lie and trick and deceive to do it, but Clea couldn't imitate her. She needed to stand squarely on her own piece of territory, know herself for what she was and be in control of herself.

If she lost the dignity of being a free agent she would lose all will. She would hate herself.

When the bedroom door clicked open she stiffened, expecting to hear Kerasteri, but her quick glance over her shoulder revealed Melissa looking half disturbed, half malicious, her black eyes very hard.

'What did Papa say to you?'

Clea flushed again. So Melissa knew? She didn't

answer, not sure how much Melissa did know, and her stepsister walked over to her, hands on her slim hips in the pleated black skirt she wore.

'I saw you with Ben on the beach.' The words shot out like an accusation, but there was an undertone of sheepish defiance about them.

Clea looked at her sharply then. 'You told your father?'

'You shouldn't have stolen Ben from me.' Melissa tossed back her black curls, her lower lip pouting, but her eyes didn't quite meet Clea's now. It was clear she was shaken by the violence with which her father had reacted.

'I didn't,' Clea said wearily. 'You can't steal what doesn't belong to anyone—I told you. And I didn't want him, anyway.'

'So I saw,' Melissa threw back spitefully.

'Oh, Mel!' Clea sighed, digging her fingernails into the soft continental quilt covering her bed.

Melissa relented, coming over to sit beside her and staring at her dubiously. 'Papa's so angry! I didn't think it would make him that mad.'

'You know him,' said Clea, in ironic acceptance. Melissa did know him, as Clea would never do. She knew her father so well because she had never needed to work out what made him tick. Her blood understood what her mind had never paused to consider.

'I thought he'd have a stroke,' Melissa confessed. 'When he came back from the beach he was like a lunatic. He went into his study and played his stereo at full volume.' She looked at Clea. 'Did you hear it?'

'No.' Clea hadn't heard anything, too absorbed in her own private struggle.

'I'm sorry,' Melissa said reluctantly, touching her arm. 'I wouldn't have told him if I'd realised how badly he'd take it. I was in a temper—I just ran off and told him on the spur of the moment.'

Clea nodded, her head bent. 'How did you come to see us?' She hadn't heard Melissa coming down to the beach or going away, but then she had been so caught up with her argument with Ben that it was doubtful if she would have heard a thunderbolt strike the trees behind them.

'I was coming down to the beach to find you. When I got back to the house, they told me you'd gone down there in the rain and I thought you were behaving pretty oddly. I stopped on the lane and I saw you and Ben. I was mad. I ran back to the house and Papa was just getting out of his car. The electricity had been cut off in Athens for a while; the storm had done some damage at the power station. So Papa had decided to come home. I just poured it out to him. I didn't stop to think, I was just so furious.'

There was no point in reproaching her, so Clea shrugged. 'It doesn't matter.'

Melissa watched her. 'What were you and Ben doing to make Papa so angry?' There was a touch of excited curiosity now.

Clea shuddered away from it. 'I don't want to talk about it.'

'I'm not shocked,' Melissa said coaxingly.

'There's nothing to be shocked about.' Clea sat up, swinging her legs over the bed. 'Can we forget it?'

'Why won't you tell me? If you don't, my imagination will run riot.' Melissa was laughing, hoping to tease her into admitting something.

'That's up to you and your imagination,' Clea said drily.

'Don't be tiresome!'

'I'm sick of the subject,' said Clea with bitterness. 'Let's drop it, shall we?'

'I knew you fancied Ben,' Melissa said, laughing, half annoyed. 'You tried hard not to show it, but I could tell.'

'I don't!' Clea's face burnt and she stiffened.

'Liar,' Melissa mocked. 'I saw you on the beach, remember. I couldn't hear what was said, but even at that distance it was obvious what was going on.'

'Leave me alone!' Clea burst out sharply, and Melissa, looking offended, shrugged and sauntered to the door.

'Do you know your trouble? You take things too seriously.' The door banged and Clea covered her face with her hands.

Melissa had put her finger on it. Clever, Clea thought grimly. It had made her sick to see the avid, excited curiosity in her stepsister's eyes. Melissa's own emotions were all surface ones: lightly aroused and largely a reflection of vanity. Melissa enjoyed the small coin of sexual relationship. She liked to flirt, to tease, to be amused. She would have enjoyed arousing Ben's passion, but she would have known how to hold him at a distance, withdraw without committing herself. Clea had nothing in common with her stepsister bar the accident of gender.

I take things too seriously, she told her reflection. Why aren't I like Melissa? She's a sapling that can bend with the storm, spring up again when it's passed over, untouched by it. I lack her ability to give way.

Melissa would marry Alexos and have children and one day she would turn into a managing, elegant Greek matron, running her home with expertise and repeating the pattern of her own life for her children if they allowed it.

Over the next few days Clea saw little of Kerasteri. He left for his office early in the morning and during that time he spent his evenings in Athens, coming home late. Clea knew he was avoiding her. It hurt, but it left her time to think.

When her mother died she had left a small sum of money in trust for Clea and Kerasteri had paid it into a bank account for her when she was eighteen. Clea was not extravagant, and she had a sizeable sum in the bank. There would be no financial problem if she went to England. She would have enough money to get there, find somewhere to live, get a job.

Having been born in England of English parents, she had a British passport, which her stepfather had insisted she should keep up to date.

'This is an uncertain world,' he had pointed out. 'Who knows? You might one day need that passport.'

Clea needed it now. She knew that if she stayed in Greece, her stepfather would try to persuade her, coerce her if need be, and she was afraid of the emotional blackmail he might bring to bear.

She had to get right away, find a world in which she might feel she really belonged. The role of the outsider is always a lonely one; Clea was tired of it.

After the storm the heatwave subsided into the usual hot Greek weather and it became possible to sleep at night again. The days were cloudless and sunny, of course, but that appalling, enervating heat had gone.

One afternoon Clea drove into Athens to do some shopping. At the back of her mind she knew she also intended to book a flight to London, but the idea disturbed her so much that she pushed it away for as long as she could.

Ermou Street was crowded, tourists shuffling along in droves, staring and exclaiming over everything they saw. Clea did her shopping without haste and made her way to the airline office.

While she was inside it she was tense and pale, afraid someone who knew her would see her there and report it to her stepfather. But she only saw strangers, tourists booking their own flights and hanging around impatiently while the clerks checked on times and connecting flights.

She was so disturbed afterwards that she walked out into the street without looking where she was going and bumped into somebody who was about to enter the office.

Clea looked up, startled, a word of apology on her lips. 'Oh!' she said huskily as she recognised Ben. Shock stiffened her whole body.

He looked as startled as she had, and his black brows drew into a straight line which gave his face a frowning hardness she had never seen in it before. 'Hello,' he said slowly. 'How did you get off the leash?'

Flushing, she turned away and he caught her arm, his fingers incisive. 'No, you don't. I want to talk to you.'

'I don't want to talk to you.' She was recovering from her first surprise now and her voice was cool and offhand.

'That's too bad, because you're going to have to,'

he muttered, holding her too tightly for her to escape without an undignified struggle. 'Come and have a drink.'

'I've got too much to do.'

People walking past glanced at them curiously, making her aware that they were blocking the pavement outside the airline office.

'You can spare me five minutes,' Ben told her drily, urging her forward. 'There's a little taverna just around this corner.'

'There always is,' said Clea, anger making her tongue sharp.

He half pushed her down the steps into the shadowy interior and the proprietor came forward to serve them. Ben ordered for her without hesitation and when they were alone again he looked at her across the little table, his expression ironic.

'You're still alive, then. I wondered if he would strangle you.'

'Thanks for the concern.' He hadn't been worried enough to find out, though, Clea noted.

'But I decided you'd survive,' he drawled. 'Kerasteri didn't strike me as the sort of guy who uses physical violence to his women.'

'No,' Clea agreed.

'Even when he's sick with jealousy.'

Clea thought for a moment she hadn't heard that properly. She stared at him, her blue eyes wide and incredulous.

Ben gave her a dry smile. 'I've hit the nail on the head, haven't I?'

'What are you talking about?' A cold shiver ran down her back. There was something in his face which bothered her.

'Oh, come on, you know what I'm talking about. He's in love with you himself.'

'No!' she broke out, so sharply that the man getting their drinks stared at her in curious surprise as he came over and placed them on the table.

Ben waited until he had gone before he said coolly: 'It may not be conscious, maybe you didn't even know yourself, but the feeling's there under the surface. He wouldn't have reacted with that sort of savagery if he hadn't been going out of his mind.'

'I won't listen, it isn't true!' Clea half rose and Ben clamped a hand on her wrist. 'Let me go!' she groaned, struggling.

He yanked her down into the seat. The man behind the bar hovered at a distance, half inclined to come over and find out what was going on between them.

'Sit there and listen,' ordered Ben in a low voice.

She sat, shivering, staring at him. There was a little silence while their eyes held. Ben had a hard glittering anger in his eyes; his whole face was alive with it.

'Did he tell you what he did? He knocked me senseless and left me on the beach. One minute we were shouting at each other, the next he clubbed me down with a blow at the back of my neck. I went down like a log.'

Clea was aghast. 'I'm sorry—did he really hurt you?'

'Oh, no,' Ben said icily. 'I just love being knocked out when I'm not expecting it.'

'He was very angry,' Clea said helplessly.

'I did notice.'

'He didn't tell me there had been a fight,' Clea said, staring at her drink.

'There wasn't any fight. I don't call it a fight when one man smashes another one down without warning.

I'll be ready for him next time he tries it.'

'There won't be a next time,' Clea muttered.

'You've come to heel, have you?' The depth of contempt in that made her wince. 'Shall I tell you what I think?'

'No, I don't want to hear.'

'I'm sure you don't, but you're going to. He wants you to himself, but he knows he can't have you, so he's handing you over to someone he can trust not to be a threat to him. From what you've told me about this Dimitri guy, he'll never stand up to Kerasteri. He won't try to come between you and your stepfather, and that's what Kerasteri wants.'

'You're sick!' muttered Clea, her teeth tight, her voice only just audible.

'I've got eyes in my head, that's all—I saw it the first time I met you. He's always touching you, watching you. And you're half scared, half in love with him yourself.'

'I won't listen,' said Clea, bending her head.

'That's why he won't let you choose a man for yourself. After you'd gone the other day he was beside himself with rage and jealousy. His language was turning the air blue.' Ben had a harsh sound to his voice, his grey eyes flinty.

'He's my stepfather!'

'What's that got to do with it? There's no blood tie and he isn't that old, is he? What is he? Late forties? And for years you've been right there under his nose, tempting him.'

'Shut up!' Clea whispered, feeling very cold. She did not want to think about what he was saying. It was an appalling idea. Kerasteri was her father in everything but blood. She looked at Ben with anguished hostility. 'Your mind is disgusting!'

'Rational,' he said curtly. 'I use my eyes. It didn't dawn on me overnight. I began to suspect it quite early on, but on the beach that afternoon he could hardly keep it out of sight. He wanted to kill me.'

'Keep your voice down,' Clea whispered. 'Do you want the whole city to hear?' The proprietor was slowly polishing his counter, his head bent, but although he wasn't looking in their direction she could sense that he was trying to catch what Ben was saying.

Ben glanced over his shoulder, then drew some coins out of his pocket and flung them on the table, getting up.

Clea got up too and walked after him. Neither of them had touched their drinks.

The brilliant sunshine flashed on to her eyes and she looked down, stumbling after Ben into the street. They paused and stood there, as though neither of them quite knew what to say.

What Ben had said just now lay between them like an act of violence against which she had barely known how to defend herself. She had been too unprepared for it. The repercussions still reverberated in her head. Her initial reaction had merely been to deny, with inarticulate shock, but as the realisation of what he thought had begun to seep into her she was growing angrier.

Huskily she told him: 'You're wrong about him, and if you think that I ...' It was too painful to say. She broke off, then at the ironic darkness of his glance started again, even more angrily. 'It isn't true, any of it. Only a sick mind would think of it. I think of him as my father.'

'Do you?' Ben's drawl doubted it.

'Yes!'

'And how does he think of you? What's he thinking when he strokes your neck and looks at you like a hungry animal?'

She started away with a low, horrified groan and he snatched at her, his hand catching her bag strap. The strap broke under his forceful grip. It slid from her hand and fell to the pavement and the catch came undone, showering the contents into the roadway.

Ben muttered irritably and knelt to pick them up. Clea knelt beside him, hurriedly shovelling things back inside without looking at him. He had halted, holding something. Clea glanced up and then whitened as she saw what he held.

'Well, well, well,' he drawled, flipping open the cardboard wallet which held her air ticket.

'Give me that!' She tried to take it from him and he held her off casually with one hand while he stared at the ticket.

'So you're going to England?' His black head lifted and he stared into her eyes.

She took the ticket from him and pushed it into her bag, rising, her face averted. As she turned away she saw a taxi and hailed it. The driver leaned out and she gave him the name of the road in which her car was parked, climbing into the back of the taxi.

Ben made no attempt to come with her. The taxi drew away and Clea stared straight ahead, her hands clenched in her lap.

CHAPTER FIVE

THAT evening, Kerasteri came home early from the office and walked into the living-room where Melissa and Clea were talking, taking them by so much surprise that they didn't speak for a moment, but stared at him. His tie was loose, his collar undone, his jacket over his arm. He looked tired, pale under his tan.

'Hello, Papa,' said Melissa, her voice surprised. 'You're early.'

'I had a headache all afternoon,' he told her, throwing his jacket down on to a chair, 'so I decided to clear out of the office.'

'Can I get you a drink?' Melissa half turned to look at Clea, as though silently asking if Clea would like to do that. The distance which Kerasteri had kept between them over the last few days had been obvious even to Melissa's indifferent, easy-going nature.

Clea moved to the decanters without saying anything. Kerasteri sank down into a chair and took off his tie, leaning back with a deep sigh.

'What have you been doing with yourselves today?' He asked Melissa with his eyes on her, but the question was phrased as though intended for both girls.

Melissa shrugged. 'Swam, shopped, met friends for lunch. The usual routine.' Her voice was heavy with boredom.

'You poor girl,' her father retorted, smiling faintly. 'What a terrible life you lead! I'm sorry for you. There

I am, leading a wonderful life, with business lunches and hours of exciting talk about finance and ways and means, and all you have to do with yourself is swim and spend money or chat with your friends. I don't know how you bear it.'

'Not sarcasm,' Melissa laughed. 'Not so early in the evening—my nerves won't stand it.' She dropped a kiss on top of his silvered head and wandered to the door. 'I'm going up to change.'

Clea turned, a glass in her hand, giving her stepsister a nervous, anxious look. She got back a wink, a gesture of the hand urging her to stay and make it up with Kerasteri. Melissa vanished before Clea could send her a silent appeal to stay.

Kerasteri stared at the polished black toe of his shoe, moving it in a small circle with apparently rapt attention. Clea took him his drink and he accepted it with a nod.

On the point of stealing off, Clea was halted when he said quietly: 'I want to apologise. I said some things to you that I regret. I was too angry to think what I was saying.'

She swallowed and answered with difficulty. 'It doesn't matter.'

'It does. I had no business saying such things to you. I know they were unfounded accusations. You aren't that sort of girl, you never have been. Any blame there was goes to him—I realise that. And I'm sorry I ever suggested such things about you.'

'Please, forget it, Papa,' Clea murmured.

'I shan't forget it for a long time.' Kerasteri lifted his glass to his mouth and swallowed some of the amber liquid. There was silence for a moment, then he said abruptly: 'I've done some checking on him.'

She was startled. 'On Ben?'

He shot her a grim stare. 'On Winter,' he agreed as though it annoyed him just to hear her use Ben's first name.

Clea was half incredulous, watching him now with her blue eyes enormous in her troubled face.

'What do you know about him?' Kerasteri demanded.

She shook her head. 'Nothing, nothing much at all.'

'His mother was Greek.'

'I remember he said so.'

'Did he tell you what sort of woman she was?' Kerasteri's full lips twisted in a hard smile as he watched her.

Clea shook her head again.

'She eloped with his father when she was sixteen. They ran off together while she was at a boarding school in England. Of course, her family found them, by then she was expecting a child and the only thing they could do was to marry her off hurriedly before it became obvious.'

'Was that ...' Clea began.

'The child was Winter,' agreed Kerasteri.

Clea stared at the sunlight dancing back at her from a stark landscape painting hanging on the opposite wall. Her own reflection was outlined on the glass covering the picture, a pale shape like that of a ghost, insubstantial and shifting, her blonde hair gleaming about her tense face.

'Not a very good beginning,' she said slowly.

'She was starting a pattern she's kept up ever since,' Kerasteri told her curtly. 'She left her husband when she was twenty-two and skipped off to the States with a business acquaintance of his. After a year with him she bolted with a painter.' He shrugged his wide shoulders. 'I gather the list is endless. She never stays with any of them long. My contact told me she was notorious for it, even though she's now in her forties.'

'How dreadful!' It sounded trite, but Clea was too shaken by the story to know what to say. She thought of Ben's hard cynical face when he told her that his mother was Greek. The cynicism was understandable now that she had heard his mother's story.

'Her son comes out of the same box.' Kerasteri finished his whisky and put down the glass with a little slam. 'I gather he goes through women at a rate of knots. I wish I'd known all this about him before I let him into my home.'

There was little Clea could say to that except to agree. She looked at her stepfather; their eyes met wordlessly and she flushed, looking away.

'If I set eyes on him again I'll break his neck!' Kerasteri stood up, his legs apart in a belligerent stance, his black head picking up the sunlight and sending off silvery rays of light. 'I'm sorry that we quarrelled over a swine like that, my little dove. I should have known the fault was entirely his. I beg your pardon.'

It was so rare for him to apologise, to admit a fault or look at her with hesitant, appealing eyes that Clea was almost in tears. She nodded without being able to say a word. Kerasteri seemed to wait for her to speak, then he came over to her and put an arm around her trembling shoulders, brushing his lips across her forehead.

'My temper ran away with me. I've always been so proud of you. You are made in your mother's image,

Clea; gentle, loving, very feminine. I couldn't take it
when I thought you had let that swine manhandle you.'

'Don't!' Clea began, her voice husky, but could
not get out another word; her throat was choked with
unshed tears.

Kerasteri patted her with clumsy affection, then hurriedly went out as though he, too, found it too moving
to be able to speak.

Clea stood there, aching with guilt and regret and
unhappiness. She did not need to be told that, despite
what her stepfather had just said, he would erupt into
further rage if she asked him to let her cry off from
her marriage. He had found out that Ben Winter was
the son of a notoriously unfaithful, amoral woman and
that he had a reputation which matched that of his
mother, and so Kerasteri had decided that all the fault
lay with Ben, but his mind would as easily swing again
if Clea told him she did not want to marry Dimitri.

His apology was based on a belief that Clea was the
submissive, feminine creature he took her to be, and
she would give the kaleidoscope of his attitudes a
further shake if she mentioned the idea of breaking
her engagement.

Melissa was delighted that evening when her father
showed every sign of being in a lively good humour.
She took it to mean that the family division was now
over and, being Melissa, she was relieved. She did not
like atmospheres in the house. Kerasteri could brood
like a thundercloud for days, bursting out with deep-
throated roars of anger whenever he was given an
opportunity. Of course Melissa's dislike of these tempers was purely personal. It meant that Kerasteri kept
a stricter eye on her too and was short-tempered all

the time. It made her uncomfortable and disrupted her busy social life.

'We must have Dimitri and Alexos to dinner next week,' Kerasteri decided cheerfully as he sipped his after-dinner brandy.

Melissa made a face at Clea across the table. 'Must we, Papa?' she dared to complain, sure that tonight he would not erupt with fury.

Kerasteri shook his forefinger at her, smiling. 'Naughty girl! Yes, you must. You don't see enough of Alexos. A pity he lives in Corinth. If he could get to Athens more often you could get to know him better.'

'I know him too well already,' Melissa moaned.

'Clea shall choose a special menu for the dinner,' Kerasteri decided, smiling at Clea. 'I think you two should do the cooking, impress them with your talents.'

'My talents don't lie in the direction of the kitchen,' Melissa said, giggling.

Her father gave her a chiding, indulgent glance. 'Not funny. Please be less childish, Melissa.'

'I'm not that either,' Melissa announced daringly, giving him a wicked look.

He shook his head at her, beginning to frown, and Melissa hurriedly subsided at the sight of his forehead wrinkling.

Turning to Clea, Kerasteri said: 'You'll see to it, Clea?' His dark eyes were liquid and warm, his smile gentle.

'Yes, of course,' said Clea, knowing that by the evening of the proposed dinner she would have left Greece. She looked down into the garden at the pines with their deep black pools of shadow, heard the pulsing rhythm of the cicadas and thought: will I ever sit here like this again? Will I ever hear Kerasteri laughing in a deep, amused way at one of Melissa's half-teasing challenges?

That thought was with her all the time over the next few days. She knew she was mentally saying goodbye to everything at the villa she loved. Of course, she would take them with her inside her memory, but that image would stay fixed like a fading photograph while the reality moved on in time, changing, growing, dying. It saddened Clea to recognise that everything changes, everything ends.

The realisation might hurt her, but it did not shake her sense of decision. Ever since the evening when her mind finally finished the equation which had been disturbing her for months, she had known she had to leave Greece. This was not her place. This way of life would never make her happy; she had to find her own place, her own way of life. The world both outside and inside Greece was changing rapidly and Clea wanted to discover herself against the background of that restless change.

On the day she left Greece she had a curious sense of unreality. She had to time her movements so that none of the maids should notice her taking a suitcase out of the house, and she was so preoccupied with thoughts of the ways and means of getting away that it was not until much later that she really began to face the fact that she had said goodbye to her past life.

She sat in the foyer at Athens Airport and stared at the polished floor, watching the passing feet and listening to the incoherent mumble of the tannoy as it announced flights and departures.

Kerasteri had brushed the top of her head as he left for work, as he always did, smiling at her, and she had wanted to say something which he might remember later and understand, but instinct had stopped her.

She had watched him walking away, her throat aching. Her coffee had had a bitter taste, the taste of unshed tears.

Someone stumbled over her hand luggage, spilling hot coffee from a plastic cup which they were carrying, and Clea glanced up in shock, startled out of her thoughts.

'Sorry,' she said automatically.

'My fault, I wasn't looking where I was going.' The woman looked ruefully at the spilt coffee on the floor.

'I'll get you another one,' Clea offered.

'No, don't bother!'

'It's no bother,' Clea assured her, getting up and going off to the counter from which coffee was dispensed. A queue of people waited at it and it was several minutes before Clea got two cups of coffee and came back, carrying them warily as people rushed past her.

'It's very good of you,' the other woman said, accepting her cup with a quick smile. She was a few years older than Clea, her hair a vibrant red with gold lights in it, her eyes slanting and green, heavily made up. 'I was dying for a coffee. I hate flying, it scares me rigid.'

'It scares me,' Clea agreed, sitting down beside her.

'Do you fly a lot?'

'No,' said Clea, her face wry. She sipped her coffee and stared at the high windows opposite them, watching the planes taxing to and fro on the tarmac outside. A fuel lorry cruised between them, the driver wearing a vivid orange jacket which caught the eye.

'I'm on my way to London,' the woman said, stretching out her legs with a sigh. 'Home,' she added, contentment in her voice.

'Have you been here on holiday?' Only now did Clea realise that she had fallen into English from the begining, as though she had been mentally rehearsing herself in her mother tongue. When the other woman fell over her hand case she had been wondering if she would manage to remember her English fluently. Her mother had spoken it to her during her lifetime, of course. When they were alone, that was what they always spoke.

'Yes, I spent a week at Vouliagmeni. All I did was lie on the beach and sun myself, but I suppose you get bored just doing that, after a while.'

Clea considered her, smiling. 'You have a beautiful tan.' The deep golden skin enhanced the slanting setting of the green eyes.

'Thanks.' Giving her a glance, the other said: 'So have you. Where have you been sunbathing?'

Clea's smile went. 'Oh, I live here,' she said, and then corrected herself. 'I did.'

'Did?' Curiosity showed in the other's eyes.

Clea shrugged. 'I'm going to London to live now.'

'To work?'

Clea nodded. 'If I can find a job,' she said, recognising that she had no particular training.

The other woman smiled at her in a friendly way. 'I'm sure you'll get a job. What sort of work are you looking for?'

'I've no idea,' Clea confessed. 'I've never worked before.'

'Good heavens!' There was amusement in the green eyes now. Holding out her hand, the other woman said: 'I'm Natalie Henderson, by the way.'

'Clea Warden,' Clea said, automatically accepting the hand and smiling.

'How come you've never had a job before?' Natalie surveyed her from head to foot as though assessing her status. 'Are you filthy rich?'

Clea laughed. 'Hardly! No, I just lived at home.' She cut the words off, wondering how much to admit. The sort of casual, pleasant questions strangers ask each other would arouse more curiosity, she realised, if she answered honestly.

Natalie stared at her with interest. 'Where are you staying in London?'

'I haven't decided,' said Clea, begining to feel scared as she thought ahead to her destination. She hadn't booked into a hotel, but surely in a city as big as London it wouldn't be hard to find a hotel room, at least for tonight?

Their flight was called and they made their way to the gate. As they talked, Natalie kept looking at her with increasing curiosity.

'You don't seem to have much idea where you're going or what you're going to do.'

Clea shrugged. 'I expect it will work out.'

'I hope so, for your sake,' said Natalie. 'London's a big city, you know. You will be careful, won't you?'

'I'm very cautious,' Clea assured her, smiling.

They separated as they boarded the plane, but no one took the seat next to Clea and after take-off Natalle came over to her to ask: 'Mind if I sit with you? I feel less scared if I've got someone interesting to talk to.'

'Oh, do,' Clea said with eagerness, because she felt she needed to have a friendly human being whom she knew on this flight into the unknown.

She had looked down from the plane window and seen the rugged green and brown of Greece far below as they took off over the sea. Now all she could see was blue waves like crinkled shimmering foil, the sun glancing off them and sending refractions of light back up to the plane. Greece had seemed to fall away from her both physically and mentally. She was nervous and disturbed and wanted her mind taken off her own feelings.

'What do you do?' she asked Natalie.

'Job-wise? I'm a model.'

Clea gave her an impressed, fascinated stare. She could believe it. The other girl had a ravishing figure and a way of walking and holding herself which was carefully groomed and deliberate.

'What sort of model?'

'Photographic. Advertising, mainly. I lie about on a mock beach in the studio and pretend to sip drinks or rub sun tan oil into my legs.'

'How exciting!'

'How boring,' Natalie said drily. 'Hour after hour of it can turn your hair grey. That's why I needed this holiday.'

'You live in London, I suppose?'

Natlie nodded. 'Yes, I've got a flat in Knightsbridge.'

Clea wasn't sure where that was, but the name rang a bell. Natalie caught her uncertain expression and laughed.

'Harrods?'

'Oh, Harrods,' Clea said, laughing.

'Everyone's always heard of Harrods. It isn't far. Kensington is a brisk walk away from my flat.'

'Do you shop at Harrods?' Clea looked at her clothes assessingly. They were casually elegant, the white cord jeans and black silk shirt striking without being formal.

'My dear girl, I can't afford Harrods clothes, and if I could I would still buy boutique stuff. You get something a bit different. I like people to remember what I wear.'

'I'm sure they do,' said Clea, although she thought it was more probably Natalie they remembered. She was stunningly attractive and had a lively personality.

'What about you? Did you live in Athens itself?'

Clea halted, warily searching for an answer. 'Outside,' she admitted at last, and Natalie eyed her with a lifted brow.

'You're very cagey. You're not running away from home, are you?' She grinned to underline that that was meant as a joke and then her grin vanished as she caught Clea's eyes. 'You are?' She sounded half incredulous.

Clea paused for a second longer before she found herself telling Natalie a brief version of the truth. Natalie listened in intrigued and incredulous fascination.

'You honestly mean to tell me that your stepfather was going to *make* you marry this guy?'

Clea nodded.

'Well, I'll be damned!' Natalie breathed. 'That's unbelievable. I don't blame you for running out on that situation.'

'What else could I do?'

'You're doing the right thing,' Natalie assured her firmly. 'I'd have done the same myself.'

'So here I am off to a city I've never seen since I was a baby,' Clea murmured, staring out of the window at the moving clouds below them.

There was a little silence and she turned to find Natalie eyeing her with a frown between her pencilled brows. 'I'm worried about you, landing yourself in London without a clue where you're going or what you're going to do.'

'I'll manage,' Clea said with more assurance than she genuinely felt.

'All the same ...' Natalie bit her lower lip, staring at her. 'Look, just for tonight, would you like to stay at my place? I've got a spare room you can have. To-morrow you can look around and find a cheap hotel, but flying in tonight you might end up sleeping on the Embankment. London isn't an easy place to find a hotel room at the height of the tourist season, you know.'

'That's very kind of you,' Clea said in grateful surprise. 'But I couldn't ...'

'Of course you can. Feel free. It's no bother to me. And I wouldn't sleep well tonight if I thought you were wandering around London with your suitcase looking for somewhere to sleep.'

'Oh, I'm sure I'll find somewhere.'

'You might,' Natalie agreed. 'But what if you don't? Wouldn't it be wiser to stay at my flat tonight and look for somewhere in the morning?'

'I don't want to impose on you,' Clea protested.

'There's no imposition. Now, don't argue. I'm determined to sleep peacefully tonight and I won't do if you don't agree to take me up on my offer.'

Clea laughed at her wry face. 'You're very kind.'

'If ever I run away to Athens and you're there you can do the same for me.'

'I will,' Clea promised, feeling a relaxation of the anxiety which had been depressing her.

'What was he like, this guy your stepfather wanted you to marry?' Natalie settled back in her seat, watching her.

'Dimitri? Very pleasant. Don't think that he was some sort of monster—he wasn't. I just didn't want to marry him and I knew I had to get away or they might try to make me.'

'You're sending shivers down my back,' Natalie shuddered. Her green eyes held teasing laughter as she asked: 'Wasn't there anyone else? If this was a novel there would be a hero lurking in the undergrowth, ready to slaughter your wicked stepfather for you.'

Clea flushed deeply, thinking of Ben, and looked away. 'No,' she said, but her voice somehow conveyed the fact that she was lying.

'No?' mocked Natalie, laughing under her breath. 'I'm beginning to read your mind. You look away when you aren't being exactly forthcoming.'

Clea forced a smile. 'There was no one who meant anything.'

'Tough luck,' said Natalie, still watching her intently. 'Maybe you'll meet someone in London. It's a big city.'

'You keep saying that, and I wish you wouldn't. You're making my blood run cold.'

'Sorry. Forget I mentioned it.' Natalie looked up with a smile to thank the stewardess as they were served with a meal in a cardboard box. Opening it, Natalie inspected it with an air of rueful disgust. 'The usual tired salad and plastic cold meat. Oh, well, I'm too hungry to care. I'd eat the box if that was all they were providing.'

Tasting her meat, Clea agreed: 'It might taste better, at that.'

Natalie laughed. 'When we get to my flat I'll make us Spanish omelette. I throw in anything handy if it's edible. It's my standby meal. There's always something you can find to chuck into an omelette.'

'Is modelling very hard work?'

Natalie shot her a dry glance. 'If you're thinking what I think you're thinking, forget it. You're not tall enough. And it's very hard work. Worrying about getting a job? Don't. You'll find something. There's always scope for a receptionist, for instance. You don't need training for that, just a level head and reasonable looks.'

'A receptionist?' Clea hadn't considered that idea. She smiled. 'That's a thought.'

'I could get you a few try-outs with photographers,' Natalie offered. 'But frankly I don't think your temperament is right. You need to be pretty tough in my job. What would you do if you got a proposition? Blush and run?'

'Very probably,' Clea agreed, sighing.

'Now I'd flatten him,' Natalie said, a faint hardness in her face. 'I'd smile and then I'd flatten him, but I'd make it a joke if I could, so that he could get up afterwards without feeling too bad about it. I'm used to that sort of approach, I can handle it.' She looked at Clea sideways, her lashes fluttering thickly. 'I just don't see you coping with the octopus approach or knowing how to bounce them off without making a big scene.'

'I'm sure you're right.' The more Clea thought about it the less she liked the idea.

Although she enjoyed Natalie's company and was fascinated by the glimpses of London life she got from her, the flight seemed endless and tiring to Clea. She was very relieved when they finally landed at Heathrow and made their way through the airport terminal to collect their luggage.

'Let's get a taxi,' said Natalie, making for the exit.

'How far is it to Knightsbridge?' Clea asked, following her with her case.

'God knows,' said Natalie. 'Seven miles?'

'Seven miles?' Clea stopped dead, her case banging the hip of a woman walking past who gave her a furious glare. 'Sorry,' she mumbled.

'Come on,' Natalie urged. 'There's the taxi rank outside.'

Clea stared out of the taxi window, absorbing the rain-blurred green fields, the grey sky, the speeding lines of traffic. 'Where's London?' she asked.

'We'll find it,' said Natalie, laughing.

When they did Clea wasn't sure she liked it much. The outskirts of the city seemed ugly and dull to her, a sprawling mass of closely packed streets gleaming wet in the thin rain. Night was falling, but it did not come with that sudden, dramatic rush with which it came to Greece. It slid in slowly over the city in a thickening veil. Street lamps glowed between the slate rooftops, their fuzzy orange haloes dimmed by rain. Clea sat on the leather seat beside Natalie and felt cold and alienated.

When they reached the centre of the city the traffic slowed their taxi to a jerky crawl. Clea watched the crowded streets with grim eyes. So many people and so many houses, she thought.

The taxi swerved to a halt eventually outside a tall, narrow house in a row of tall, narrow houses. Clea followed Natalie out of the taxi and stood on the pavement, staring around her in dazed disbelief. The rain still fell, fine and chilly, running down her cheek like tears.

Natalie paid the driver and Clea said as she turned away: 'Let me pay half of the fare.'

'Rubbish,' Natalie said cheerfully. 'I'd have taken the taxi anyway.'

'But all the same . . .' Clea began.

'Forget it,' Natalie urged, smiling brightly at her. 'Here we are, anyway. What do you think of Knightsbridge?'

They had passed Harrods and Clea had stared at it, impressed by the size of it. There were no such vast stores in Athens.

'Give me time to decide,' Clea murmured, picking up her case. She walked up the steps to the front door and Natalie opened it, waving her into the house. It was very quiet. As the heavy front door closed Clea stood in the hall listening for sounds of other human life in the house, but none came.

'There are three flats,' Natalie told her. 'Mine is upstairs.' She began to mount the stairs with Clea keeping close beside her, giving curious, nervous glances around her. The hall was painted white and had obviously been modernised. The high ceilings and stucco decorations suggested that it was a much older building than the present furnishing would indicate.

Natalie opened a door at the top of the flight of stairs and switched on a light. Clea walked past her into the narrow hall which the light revealed. Natalie joined her, closing the outer door with a snap. There was a sound of music somewhere. Clea heard it and looked at Natalie in surprise and enquiry. Did someone else share the flat with her?

Without a flicker of expression Natalie opened a door to the left and waved for Clea to go into the room.

Automatically, Clea obeyed, and then stopped dead as she saw the man leaning back casually in a chair on the opposite side of it. The low sound of jazz piano music went on pulsing rhythmically. The man had a long thin cigar between his fingers. Smoke from it curled up into the air. He looked different here in London. His dark suit was elegant, immaculate; his white shirt, striped blue, had a city air. The thick black hair was brushed into a smooth cap.

But it was undoubtedly Ben, and she stared, her face whitening in shock and disbelief.

'Hello, Clea,' he drawled at last, his deep voice full of mockery and a peculiar amused satisfaction.

CHAPTER SIX

'WHAT are you doing here?' Her mind was whirling with questions. What was he doing in Natalie's flat? Obviously he must know her, but how incredible, what bitter irony that Clea had managed to meet one of Ben's friends.

'Surprise, surprise!' Natalie said, laughing.

Ben didn't say anything, but lay back in the chair, his long legs stretched out casually, watching Clea with relaxed amusement.

Mushroom clouds of suspicion and anxiety began to form inside her head. Was it a complete coincidence? Ben wasn't surprised to see her. As she looked across the room, stunned, Ben had leaned back with that cool mocking smile and there hadn't been a shred of surprise in his face.

'Pleased, Ben? Aren't I the clever one?' Natalie asked, and Clea looked round at her, probing her laughing face.

'You're a witch,' Ben drawled, blowing smoke into drifting white rings and watching them lazily as they dissolved into the air. 'Was it hard to persuade her to come back here with you?'

'Easy as taking candy off a baby.' Natalie grinned round at Clea, who wasn't moving, listening and beginning to feel very worried.

'Apt description,' drawled Ben, his eyes narrowed as he watched Clea's revealing face.

'She hadn't even thought of booking a room in a hotel,' Natalie said with amused disgust. 'Would you believe it? She was going to arrive in London late in the evening without a clue where to go or how to get anywhere. If I hadn't brought her back here she would have ended up sleeping on a park bench.'

'How . . .' Clea began, and Natalie grinned at her.

'I wondered how long it was going to take you to work it out. You've been standing there with your mouth open almost since you walked into the room.' It appeared to amuse her, her green eyes were dancing.

'Did you lure me here?'

'Lure?' Natalie repeated the word, her brows arching in comic mockery. 'Cut the drama. I brought you here for Ben, that's all.'

'Ben told you to?' Clea was thinking back over their meeting at the airport, the spilt coffee, the casual smiles. Had all that been planned?

Natalie shrugged as if leaving that to her own imagination, and Clea was stung with fury.

'You lied to me!'

'There was no lying involved. I just omitted to mention that I was a friend of Ben's. You didn't ask, so I didn't need to tell you any lies.'

'The whole thing was a lie. You're a fraud! You tricked me into coming here.'

'There's gratitude for you,' Natalie muttered, beginning to look annoyed. 'I was doing Ben a good turn. You'll thank me for it some day.'

'Thank you?' Clea repeated furiously. Anger was jamming her nerve-ends, making her skin tingle with stabs of pain. Natalie had been a fraud, her friendliness and warmth a mere pretence meant to coax her into coming to the flat. Clea had trusted her without a moment's hesitation and now she felt sick.

'Thanks, Natalie,' said Ben, getting up and stubbing out his cigar with a rough movement. 'But would you mind?'

'Thanks, but get lost?' Natalie teased, her green eyes sparkling. Clea got the impression she was enjoying the whole thing, amused by Clea's dazed astonishment.

'Clea and I have some talking to do,' Ben agreed flatly.

'Now there's a new name for it,' Natalie drawled.

Clea stiffened, drawing a quick, fierce breath. What did Natalie think was going to happen, or could she guess? What had Ben told her?

'On your way, Natalie. I'll see you later,' Ben was saying, almost pushing Natalie towards the door.

'Don't fret, I'm on my way,' Natalie told him.

'I'm not staying here,' Clea said angrily, moving towards the door.

Ben's hands bit into her shoulders. 'You're not going anywhere.'

Natalie laughed. 'Enjoy yourselves,' she said, walking away.

Panic raced through Clea as she saw Natalie going. She opened her mouth to yell and Ben's hand clamped down over it, silencing her. Her body strained to break free of his, her wide, frightened eyes fixed on Natalie's back, begging her helplessly to turn round, to do something.

Natalie vanished. The door closed. Clea heard the outer door slam and Ben's hand released her mouth. She gave a hoarse cry for help, wrenching free from his restraint at the same time. She tore out of the room to the front door. The sound of Ben's footsteps slowly followed. Clea was tugging at the door, but it wouldn't budge.

'It's locked,' Ben said drily behind her.

She turned, trembling. 'I'll scream until someone hears me!'

'The house is empty—the builders have just moved out of it after modernising it and the new tenants haven't taken over the flats. There's no one to hear you, Clea.'

'I'm not staying here!'

'Oh, yes, you are.' There was no mistaking the grating hardness of his voice. 'Get that into your head here and now.'

Clea felt perspiration spring out on her palms. 'Why have you brought me here?'

He smiled, not answering. Clea's heart missed a beat at the slow sensual stare which swept over her.

'Come back in here,' he murmured, waving a hand towards the room behind him. 'There's no point in your standing there. You can't get out and you look as if you need to sit down.'

She shook her head, backing. Ben shot forward and took hold of her wrist, dragging her, struggling, back into the room. He released her there and she fled to the other side of it, staring at him.

'How did Natalie know who I was?' she asked, suddenly thinking of that.

'I planted her at the airport to pick you up.' Ben was grinning now, satisfaction in his eyes. 'I'd managed to get a snatched photo of you—a photographer went down to the villa and snapped you on the beach one morning.'

Clea winced at the surreptitious picture of a man watching her, taking pictures of her from hiding.

'I gave it to Natalie so that she could pick you out,' he added.

'You planned the whole thing,' Clea said slowly.

'I had to leave it to her how she hooked herself on to you, but Natalie's clever and she's a good actress. I just told her to get you here, whatever she had to do to achieve it.'

'What a vile, despicable trick!'

'Needs must,' Ben drawled, but his brows had drawn together and his smile had gone.

'Can't you see the whole scheme was disgusting?'

'I had to get you here,' Ben bit out. 'You wouldn't have come any other way.'

'So you tricked me,' she retorted, her eyes hating him.

'I'd no other choice.'

'Oh, yes, you did. You knew I didn't want to see you again and you should have left it at that.'

'Like hell,' Ben said fiercely, and Clea stared at the tanned, powerful lines of his face. She saw the self-involved, self-willed determination of a man who is ready to do anything to get what he wants, whatever the consequences for someone else.

He moved closer, the grey eyes flickering with an emotion she couldn't pretend she didn't understand. 'I've thought of very little else but you ever since I met you. You've got right under my skin, Clea. I wasn't letting you walk out of my life once I'd found you. No way.'

'I've no intentions of staying here.'

'It's my intentions that count,' said Ben, his eyes

brooding on her and a faint unsteadiness in his voice.

Her skin burnt at the increasing sensuality in his stare. His words were an unleashed threat which was the more alarming for being delivered with that husky emotion.

She shook her head dumbly, shivering. Ben was beside her now, looking down at her. 'You know you want to stay, Clea,' he whispered. 'You want what I want, but you just won't admit it, even to yourself.' He touched her cheek, his fingers running possessively down to her throat, leaving a trail of fire over her cold skin. 'I had to force you to admit how you felt,' he went on softly.

'No!' Clea stammered, trying not to tremble but desperately aware of the sensual brush of his fingertips.

'Don't lie to yourself,' said Ben, his mouth twisting.

'It's you who's the liar. You and that girl tricked me here. Don't try to tell yourself I wanted to come!'

'You're refusing to admit to yourself what you want. You're a coward, Clea. You're afraid of facing up to the feelings inside you.'

Clea pushed his exploring hand away and twisted her body to escape from his oppressive nearness. 'I can't understand how Natalie could trick me like that. It was a despicable thing to do!'

'I told her you were being stubborn about things,' Ben admitted. 'Natalie only knew what I'd told her.'

'And you lied to her?'

He gave a wry grimace. 'Not exactly.'

Clea guessed that he had given Natalie the impression that there was a much longer acquaintance between them than was actually the case. Perhaps Natalie had genuinely thought she was bringing estranged lovers back together. Clea looked at Ben with distaste.

'How could you?' she burst out.

'I had to get you here,' Ben muttered, his skin taking on an angry red. 'Clea, I know we haven't known each other long, but sometimes it happens like that. I fancied you that first evening. I was taken aback when Melissa's sister turned out to be a long-legged blonde with big blue eyes.' He gave her a coaxing little smile. 'I suppose it was the surprise of that that made me keep looking at you. And the more I looked, the more I liked what I saw.'

'I wish I could say the same,' Clea bit back, still furious with him.

Faint amusement showed in his eyes. 'Can't you?' he asked very softly, his mouth curving upwards.

Her heart undeniably missed a beat. It shook her to realise it, and it made her angrier. She didn't want to find the lazy charm of his smile that seductive—especially at this moment.

'I'm not staying here in this flat with you, so forget it,' she insisted, hoping she sounded firmer than she felt.

Impatience flared in the grey eyes. 'For God's sake, this isn't Greece. Who do you think is going to care? People in London don't ask questions like that. Even if they were certain you were sleeping with me they wouldn't dream of making any comment.'

'I care,' said Clea. 'I'm not going to stay, Ben.'

'Aren't you just?' he drawled, a sudden crooked humour in the line of his mouth.

'You're not laying a finger on me!' snapped Clea, backing.

'How are you going to stop me?' His eyes were alight with a mocking, excited elation which sent a shiver down her back. 'We're all alone here, Clea.' He had lowered his voice to a soft whisper. 'What do you think you're going to do to stop me?'

'You must be hard up for a woman if you have to rape one,' Clea said contemptuously.

Ben didn't like that at all. His eyes flashed. 'It won't be rape!'

'It's going to have to be!'

They stared at each other, a dangerous anger between them, their eyes fighting in a silent duel.

Ben's eyes brooded angrily, his hands clenching at his sides. For a moment she thought he was going to lose his temper outright, then he visibly forced himself to relax.

Smiling at her, he said: 'You underrate me, Clea.' His grey eyes mocked her. 'And you underrate yourself. I've no intention of raping you. Because sooner or later you're going to realise you want me as much as I want you. I think you know that already. That's why you're so angry. You don't want to admit it—but you're going to.'

'Whatever you get from me you're going to have to use force to get, and if that's going to give you any satisfaction, I'm sorry for you,' Clea said bitterly.

'Be sorry for yourself,' Ben snapped, getting angry again. 'You're turning down more than just a love affair, you know. You're scared of life itself.'

'You're just shooting a line,' said Clea, giving him a cold stare. 'I may not be very sophisticated by London standards, but I know a line when I hear it. I'm not letting you talk me into bed.'

'Who said anything about talking?' Ben watched her through his dark lashes, but she refused to let that teasing little smile do a thing to her.

'I ran away from home because I refused to be treated like a puppet. I'm a woman, not an object. If I let you talk me into bed I'd be letting you treat me like an object, too. And I won't let you do that to me. I can't stop you if you use force. You're stronger than me. But believe me, Ben, I won't make it easy for you by giving in.'

Ben's hands framed her face, tilting her head back. 'I know you're a woman, Clea,' he said huskily, staring down at her with passionate intensity. 'Do you think I would hurt you? Can't you see how much I want you?'

Her eyes stayed on his taut face, nervously reading the emotion in it. His fingers were trembling slightly as they caressed her face, his eyes burned with fixed absorption as he stared down at her. He didn't need to tell her that he wanted her. His body was tense with it and she knew her own body was shaking with an unwanted response.

'Don't,' she whispered, afraid of something which she refused to name to herself.

'Life's too short to waste, Clea. We can't throw away our chances of happiness when they come.' Bending, he began to brush his mouth over her eyes so that she had to close them. His lips played with her lashes, giving her butterfly kisses which made her tingle with angry pleasure.

'Stop it!'

'You don't want me to stop,' said Ben, a smile in his voice. 'Your skin's like a peach, did you know that?

That beautiful golden colour is going to look very out of place in London. Everywhere you go, men are going to flip over you.' His mouth was delicately sliding down her cheek and she knew he was going to reach her lips in a moment. One of his arms had closed round her waist. Clea put her hands against his shoulders to push him away, trembling from head to foot, but as she did so, Ben closed his mouth over her own with a sharp groan.

Her fingers tensed, curling into his shoulders. Ben parted her lips with a rough murmur of deep satisfaction and as his kiss deepened into demand, Clea found herself taken over by a fierce pulsating excitement which her mind couldn't control. His body moved against hers as if he wanted to imprint her with the muscled tension of chest, waist, thigh. A hand at her back pressed her closer, deepening that imprint. She could hear the rapid thud of his heart against her breasts and her own heart raced into delirium. Her fingers moved and she felt his skin beneath her palms. The next moment her arms were round his neck and her mouth was clinging heatedly to his.

She had told herself that she wouldn't let him force any response out of her, but Ben hadn't needed to use force. Her body was helplessly melting under his touch, her limbs plastic and yielding in his arms. With her eyes closed she stopped trying to think and gave way to feeling, letting the erupting lava of her desire pour up her body and cloud her brain with the fumes of passion.

Ben drew away at last, his face deeply flushed, his breathing thick and rapid. She clung to him, her eyes closed, her mouth parted, her heart drowning her head.

She heard the elated sound Ben gave and her eyes flew open. He looked at her with glittering triumph.

'Now will you admit it?' he asked, smiling like a man who has proved his point.

Clea felt sick. She looked at the flushed, hard-boned face and hated both herself and him. Her shaken head merely made him laugh, his face still full of that elated satisfaction.

'You know you want me,' he said huskily. 'I just made you admit it. If it makes you feel more virtuous to refuse to put it into words, go ahead. I don't give a damn whether you're prepared to say it or not. I know I'm right.'

'Of course, you would be,' Clea muttered.

'I am,' he said, his smile mocking.

'I'm not going to bed with you,' she insisted through her clenched teeth, her jaws aching with tension.

'Why are women such damned hypocrites?' Ben asked with a cooling stare. The elation had faded from his face but now he looked irritable. 'You're all the same; pretending reluctance until the last minute, making men go through a charade of begging on their knees just so that you can have some sort of excuse for what you want to do all the time.'

'I'm not like that!' Clea broke out.

'All women are like that. Very few of them are honest enough to admit what they want. They insist on playing the wronged innocent right up to the minute they take their clothes off.'

Clea slapped his face so hard her palm stung. Ben jerked backward, then looked at her with a dangerous rage, his lips a straight hard line, his cheek dark red where she had slapped it.

'Do that again, you little bitch, and I'll slap you right back,' he promised harshly.

Clea felt her body trembling in a terrified reaction, as though her shock and fear had caught up with her at last and were expressing themselves in an uncontrollable physical weakness. She swayed and Ben muttered under his breath, putting an arm round her.

'You're not going to pass out, are you?' He sounded irritated, impatient. She had her eyes closed and her body slackened in his arm. A chill mist was swirling through her head. She was afraid she would fall and clung to Ben's shirt, her fingers grasping it, the warmth of his skin making her even more aware of her own coldness.

'Clea,' Ben said somewhere a long way off. She was slowly sliding down when he caught her up and she felt she was floating, weightless, her head thrown back over his arm.

She heard him swearing under his breath. Her head was going round as though she were on a merry-go-round, her ears singing with the pulse of her own blood.

Ben carried her somewhere, his strides rapid. She felt him lower her to something soft which gave under her weight. He stooped over her, rubbing her cold hands.

'Hell's bells!' he muttered to himself, his tone rough.

Clea's lashes fluttered. She tried to open her eyes and Ben caught the little movement. 'Are you all right?' He sounded anxious, impatient. 'Clea, for God's sake!'

She looked at him through her lashes. He was frowning, his face disturbed.

Clea recognised that she had achieved some slight advantage. Ben was worried, genuinely anxious now, watching her with that frown above his grey eyes.

Weakly she whispered: 'What happened?' She made her voice issue in a faint way.

'You fainted,' he told her, leaning towards her. He was still rubbing her hands in an ineffective way. 'You're as white as a sheet. How do you feel?'

'I'm so tired,' she breathed.. 'The flight ... it's all been a terrible strain ...'

'Of course,' he said, his brow clearing slightly. 'You must have left Athens hours ago. Are you hungry? Can I get you something to eat?'

She shook her head slowly. 'If I could only get some sleep,' she whispered.

'Sleep,' he said, as though hearing the word for the first time. 'Yes, of course. You're very cold. I suppose the change in temperature must be responsible for that.'

Clea shivered. Ben lifted her again and slid her, fully dressed, into the bed, covering her with a thick continental quilt. 'Would you like some extra blankets? There are some in the linen cupboard.'

'Yes, please, if it's no trouble.'

'Of course not,' he said, turning.

She waited until he was out of the room before she leapt out of the bed and shot to the door. Her heart hammered as she inspected the handle and a sense of deep relief sang inside her as she found the bolt. She thrust it home and heard an exclamation from Ben in the hallway.

He was back at the door a second later, rattling the

handle and then pounding on it with his clenched fist.
'Open this door!'

'No,' Clea said, facing it and hoping her voice
sounded cool.

'You treacherous little bitch!' Ben growled. 'Clea,
open this door! Do I have to break it down?'

'Yes,' she said, wondering if the door would stand
up to the battering he was giving it. It looked solid
enough, but it was shivering under the impact of his
blows, the panels resounding.

'I should have known better than to trust a woman,
even when she's as white as a sheet and looks as if she's
at death's door,' Ben muttered. 'Clea, don't make me
angry with you.'

She walked back to the bed and got into it, fully
dressed still. She wasn't taking off a stitch of clothing
while Ben was around. She pulled the quilt over her
shoulders and watched the door, listening as Ben
crashed against it and then gave a grunt of pain.

'Damnation!' he muttered on a gasp. 'I think I've
broken my shoulder.'

Clea yawned loudly. 'I'm going to sleep. Goodnight,
Ben.'

There was silence outside. She could hear him
breathing close to the door. What was he thinking?
she wondered. Even more important, what was he
planning in that convoluted head of his?

'Darling,' he whispered huskily. 'You're just being
obstinate and you aren't thinking straight. Just now
when I kissed you, you couldn't hide the way you felt,
any more than I could.'

Clea didn't answer, curling up under the quilt, listening to him and torn between hating him and a peculiar,

nagging pleasure at the emotion she could hear in his voice.

There was a pause, then he said brusquely: 'Is it your stepfather? I thought you were leaving because you realised how impossible that was.'

Clea's face grew hot. 'Don't start that again!'

'You wouldn't get so angry if you didn't know I'd hit on the truth,' Ben challenged, his voice muffled by the door between them.

'I've only ever thought of him as my father, and it makes me ill to hear you say things like that.'

'Very well,' Ben said, conceding that hurriedly. 'I'll believe that. It was all on his side. You wouldn't have run if you hadn't suddenly realised ...'

'I suddenly realised that both of you were treating me as if I had no value except as something you wanted, something for you to dispose of, like a work of art. Well, I'm not a disposable object. I'm a human being with my own value. I want to decide my own life. I want some self-respect, some integrity. I won't be used and controlled like a child!'

'I don't think of you as a child.' Ben had husky laughter in his voice, but Clea didn't smile.

'You certainly don't think of me as an adult or you wouldn't have tried to trick me here. You just talked about women with contempt. I listened to everything you said and it all underlined the truth about the way you see me. You despise women. You use them and get what you can out of them, but you put no value on them at all.'

'Don't be absurd,' he said, the laughter gone and anger in his voice again.

'Go away,' Clea begged, tiredness making her head ache. 'You make me sick!'

She turned on to her face and hid it in the pillow, pulling the quilt right up to her ears. Ben talked softly and persuasively next to the door for a while, but Clea wasn't listening. She refused to listen. There was nothing Ben could say to which she wanted to listen.

CHAPTER SEVEN

ALTHOUGH she was so tired Clea didn't think she would sleep; her nerves were too jumpy. She lay listening to the silence in the flat and wondering what Ben was doing. The windows were double-glazed, shutting out the sounds from the street below. The glow of a street lamp made a moving circle on the wall and she watched it, her eyes hot and weary.

She couldn't keep them open. They kept closing and then she would jerk awake again and look around her with agitated glances as though expecting to find Ben in the room with her.

The heavy quilt was slowly bringing warmth back to her stiff limbs. It relaxed her and she steadily stretched under it, yawning. Although Ben couldn't see her she felt it was essential that she stay alert, awake, in case he tried to get into the room again.

It nagged away at her that she had let his lovemaking arouse her. That would only have given him encouragement. Clea hated herself for weakening. She hated him for having made it impossible for her to resist the hungry pressure of his mouth, the tight possession of his arms. Every time she visualised that elated satisfaction in his face she felt a slow burning fury inside her. Damn him! she whispered, and the silent room seemed to echo the words mockingly.

That was her last conscious thought. She didn't remember sliding into a troubled sleep, but she must have done, because the next time she opened her eyes the room was full of daylight and the sun was shifting around the walls in a shower of golden dust.

Clea sat up warily. Her own reflection came back at her from the mirror on the dressing-table opposite. Her flushed features and tousled hair bore witness to the hours she had slept and the twisting uneasiness of her body during that sleep.

My clothes will be unwearable, she thought, grimacing. Crumpled, untidy, her appearance wasn't going to turn any man on at this hour in the morning.

She listened, but couldn't hear a sound from the flat. Was Ben asleep? She slid out of the bed and tip-toed to the door. Bending, she put an ear against it, intent on the slightest sound, but could hear none.

The loudest sound she could hear was the beat of her own heart. She straightened, wondering what to do. Her case was in the hall, where she had left it when she first arrived. She couldn't even change her crumpled clothes.

Letting her glance wander round the room, she noted the pale pink vanity unit in one corner. She could at least wash. But if she turned on the water Ben might hear it and be aware that she was awake, and that Clea did not want.

If Ben was asleep she had a chance of getting out of here before he heard her. She silently slid back the bolt and held the door slightly ajar, ears pricked.

Not a sound. She drew the door back and poised, ready to spring back into the room if Ben appeared. There was no sign of him and the flat had an empty feel. It gave back that peculiar dead sound which places have when there is no one there.

Moving like a stealthy cat, Clea made her way along the narrow hall towards the flat front door. Her heart was hammering against her breastbone and she was tense from head to foot.

'Going somewhere?'

The cool voice made her jump as if she'd been shot, spinning round to find Ben leaning on the sitting-room door in a lazy attitude, his eyes mocking.

Clea felt her tension snap. She wanted to scream, but could only stare at him in bitter silence.

He looked as calm as though he had nothing on his mind; his clothes were immaculate, his black hair brushed back from that handsome, amused face.

'Slept well?' he enquired, lifting one brow.

'Damn you!' Clea stammered, too choked to say anything else.

He laughed under his breath. 'Still in a temper? I though a good night's sleep might have made you more reasonable.'

'I suppose you slept like an angel,' Clea flung back with a savage rage against him making her voice harsh.

'Do angels sleep? That's a moot point. I'd have said it was one of those theological problems that keep people arguing for centuries, like how many angels can sit on the point of a pin.'

'Very funny,' Clea snapped.

His eyes were moving over her, his brows raised in dry comment. 'You look as though you spent the night in a haystack.'

'I feel as though I had,' she muttered. Her glance moved aside in search of her suitcase. 'Where are my things?'

'Here,' he said lifting the case from a chair. 'Would

you like to shower and change before breakfast?'

'Yes,' said Clea, snatching it from him.

'Naughty!' he mocked, taking it back. 'I'll take it to your room for you. You're my guest, remember.'

'Guest?' She was almost speechless at that.

He laughed again. 'In a manner of speaking.'

'I'm a prisoner, not a guest!'

'Don't let's spend hours arguing over definitions,' Ben reproached her with amusement. He carried the case down the hall, sauntering so casually that she followed him without thinking.

'Hungry?' he asked as he put the case down on the bed.

'Starving,' she admitted, her stomach reminding her that she hadn't eaten for hours. The cold food on the aeroplane was merely a distant and not very pleasant memory.

'What would you like? Egg and bacon? Tea or coffee?'

'Anything that's available,' said Clea, half groaning. She stopped, looking at him in sharp interest. 'Who's doing the cooking?'

He read the thought behind the question and smiled at her with that teasing amusement again. 'I am, so don't get all excited.'

She slackened from the faint hope of escape which had entered her head, turning her face away from him with a frown.

'And don't scowl,' Ben added with faint impatience, turning towards the door. 'Breakfast will be ready in a quarter of an hour. Can you be ready by then?'

She nodded and he went out. Clea bolted the door. Ben paused and said softly through it: 'Even when you're looking as though you've been sleeping in a hay-stack you're still fantastic, Clea.'

Her heart skipped. She didn't answer and heard him walk away after a moment, as though he had waited for her to say something.

She opened her case and got out a pair of jeans and a thin cotton sweater, clean underclothes and a towel. Stripping off her clothes, she went into the shower cubicle beside the vanity unit and turned on the jets. For a few seconds the spray was ice cold and she shuddered in shock at it, then it warmed enough to be bearable. Clea took her time in washing. She felt sticky and uncomfortable after that night; her whole body seemed to have been bathed in perspiration.

When she had dressed again she felt easier. She brushed her damp hair and then did her make-up, taking care to give some semblance of normality to her face. She felt like someone putting on armour before a battle. She needed a shield to keep Ben at a distance.

Ben was in the kitchen at the far end of the flat. Clea could hear the bubbling of a percolater, the sound of spitting fat, the movement of someone working quickly. A delicious odour of bacon was filling her nostrils as she walked into the room.

Sunlight flooded it, and Ben's hair glinted in that brilliance. He glanced at her over his shoulder, flicking a glance from her tight white sweater to her jeans.

'Very neat,' he mocked.

'Can I do anything to help?' Clea was trying to place their relationship on a casual footing now. If she could only get Ben to realise that he was treating her with contempt she might make him let her go.

'Thanks,' he said, sliding eggs on to a warmed plate. 'Could you find some cups and saucers? The coffee is ready.'

'It smells fantastic.' Her stomach was clamouring for food and the mingled scents of coffee and bacon were intoxicating. She opened several cupboards before she found cups. Ben was placing their food on the table. A glass of chilled orange juice stood next to each plate. Clea brought the coffee pot over and poured coffee while Ben sat down at the table and sipped his juice.

'A beautiful morning,' Ben pointed out, glancing at the window.

'Yes.' Clea looked at the sky too. Small fluffy white clouds drifted through the blue, but they didn't look like rain clouds.

She didn't say anything more for a few minutes, drinking her juice and then beginning on her meal with appreciation. Ben ate, his black head bent, before looking at her through his lashes.

'Did you leave a note?' he asked.

'What?' Clea looked up, eyes wide.

'For Kerasteri.'

She flushed. 'No.' She hadn't even thought of it. She had been too scared and too eager to get away before he realised she had gone.

'My God!' Ben exclaimed, his face sharp. 'He'll be out of his mind! You'd better write to him today.'

Clea felt sick. She had thoughtlessly vanished without giving her stepfather any clue as to where she was going or what might be happening to her. It didn't please her that it should have been Ben who pointed that out to her.

She slowly nodded. 'Yes, I must do that.'

'How could you?' Ben watched her, his grey eyes flinty. 'You must have known it would tear him to shreds. You might at least have posted him a note just to let him know you were safe.'

A spark of anger lit inside her. 'You've made your point. I'll admit I should have done.'

Ben had a peculiar intent expression. 'Did you want to make him sweat?'

She flushed more deeply, her head bent. 'Of course not.'

'I wonder,' he muttered, a faint savagery in his voice. 'Women like to use their claws.'

'Why do you always generalise about women as though they were all identical? They're not.'

'Ah, but they are,' Ben drawled, picking up his coffee cup and sipping it.

'You prefer to believe they are, that's all.'

'I speak as I've found.'

'If you treat all women with contempt and indifference that isn't very surprising!'

'Indifference?' He put down his cup and gave her a wicked, teasing smile. 'Wrong word, Clea. When have I ever treated you with indifference?'

Her teeth met. 'That depends on your definition of the word.'

'Oh, we're back to definitions, are we? You seem to have a passion for them. It must be your Greek upbringing. They've always loved to argue about the exact meaning of every word in the dictionary.'

'I'm not getting into a wrangle over meanings,' said Clea, returning to her breakfast.

For a while they ate in silence again. Ben finished

his meal and leaned back, drinking a second cup of coffee, watching her with narrowed eyes.

'What exactly did you plan to do when you got to London?' he asked.

'Get a job.'

'As?'

'A receptionist,' said Clea without thinking, and that brought Natalie back into her mind. She looked at him directly. 'You called Natalie a friend of yours. What did that mean, exactly?'

She caught the flash of comprehension in his eyes and he gave her a wry, mocking little smile. 'Jealous?'

She stiffened. 'No, I'm not.'

'No?' He openly doubted that, his eyes amused.

'She was ... involved with you?' Clea asked dryly.

He shrugged. 'It was years ago—four years ago, to be precise. We had a brief thing together, but it didn't work out. Natalie's very attractive, but we hadn't much in common.'

Clea looked away, refusing to admit to herself that it hurt her to know that Natalie and Ben had once been that close. Lovers, she thought angrily. Why not use the word? She knew Ben well enough by now to realise that the relationship would not have been platonic; he was only interested in one relationship with a woman.

Ben was looking around the room, his face casual and unconcerned. 'This was her flat, actually.'

Clea felt a streak of pain and anger rush through her. 'Natalie's flat? This is Natalie's flat?' Somehow that made it all far worse.

'Not now,' Ben said calmly. 'I own the whole house. Natalie moved out six months ago when I got the builders in to do the place up. She's got a flat in 'Chelsea now. She's living with an actor—they've been together for months now. I think it may be serious.'

'My God,' Clea muttered, not knowing whether to laugh or cry. 'They've been living together for months and you think it may be serious?'

Ben regarded her, his mouth crooked. 'Face it, Clea, this is another world, another time. You've got to learn the rules or you won't survive in it for long.'

'Whose rules?' Clea demanded. 'Yours? I'll live by my own rules, thank you, or I won't live at all.'

'We can never live entirely by our own rules. Society won't let us.'

'How can it stop us? If you're talking about the law, okay, we may have to abide by that. But we don't have to do anything we don't want to do if there's no law forcing us.'

He sighed, looking irritated. 'I'm talking about the social attitudes of everyone around us. People today don't expect you to live the life of a monk just because you aren't married.'

'I don't care what people expect or otherwise!'

'The pill's liberated women from marriage,' Ben said shortly.

'You mean it's liberated men,' Clea retorted. 'They don't have to bother to accept responsibility for women any more. There's no more risk of getting a girl pregnant. Men can just waltz in and out of beds without stopping to think.'

'You keep talking about being a person, having value as a human being and being respected as yourself. If you meant a word of that you wouldn't want a man taking responsibility for you.'

'I don't want you taking responsibility for me,' she insisted, getting annoyed. 'I want you to admit that I have the choice as to whether I go to bed with you or not.'

'I'd agree with that,' Ben said through his teeth, 'if I thought you knew what you were doing, but you don't. You're turning down something you haven't got a clue about. And you're doing it for the wrong reasons.'

'Who are you to say whether my reasons are wrong or right?'

'I'm a man who's crazy about you,' said Ben, his eyes suddenly gleaming with amusement. 'And I refuse to let you get away from me until you've faced up to what you feel about me.'

'There's something crooked about that thinking,' Clea said defiantly. 'You seem to think that you know more about my feelings than I do.'

He laughed huskily. 'I do.'

'No, you just think you do.'

He reached over the table in an abrupt movement and picked up her hand before she could withdraw it, then bending his black head over it he kissed the warm palm lingeringly.

Clea felt pleasure shoot up her arm, travelling like electricity in her blood. Her skin grew heated and when Ben looked up she couldn't quite meet his stare.

'See what I mean?' he mocked.

She jerked her hand away and stood up. 'I'll wash up.' She was furiously aware that she was trembling. Her brain might tell her that Ben's casual contemptuous attitude for women was a barrier between them, but her emotions, her body, seemed more and more to want to leap that barrier, whatever the consequences.

The more he touched her the more she had to struggle against herself.

Ben helped her clear the table and while she washed, he dried, his movements quick and deft.

Afterwards she looked at him with as much calmness as she could muster. 'Now I want to leave, Ben.'

He smiled drily. 'You know the answer to that.'

'You can't keep me here for ever.'

'I won't need to.'

She hated the cool confidence with which he said that, his smile twisted.

'You must be mad!' she snapped, her body taut. 'You haven't thought about what you're doing.'

'I've thought of little else.' His grey eyes darkened as he stared at her, his cheekbones hardening as though he was fighting for self-control. The arrogance of his face tightened into a tough mask, his mouth very straight.

'If you've got any sense you won't provoke me into showing you,' he muttered.

Clea inwardly shrank back from that glance, those rough words. She moved to the door without another word and went back to the bedroom and bolted herself safely inside it.

She couldn't stay there for ever, though, and her mind worried at the problem like a dog with a bone. How was she going to get away? She tried the window, but found it locked tight. She could break the glass, she thought, and scream for help. There was no hope of climbing out of this window, though. There was no way for her to get out through there.

The street seemed empty and quiet. She found it odd to look out over London, yet hear so little of it.

The double-glazing excluded the worst of the noise of the London traffic swirling past the end of the road. Clea could see chimneys, rooftops, spires and office blocks in the distance. A helicopter clattered through the sky. She watched it disappear and felt abandoned, lost.

At last she lay down on the bed and shut her eyes. Although she had slept last night her mind had been too tormented to let her body rest easily, and she still felt exhausted.

When Ben tapped on the door later she woke up with a start and lay there wondering for a second where she was, only to remember and close her eyes again with a little groan.

'Clea!' Ben sounded impatient.

She didn't answer. Staring up at the ceiling, she watched the sunlight dancing around the fringed lampshade.

'Clea! Clea, open this door! It's lunchtime and I've got a meal ready. Come and eat your lunch.'

Clea put her arms behind her head and stared at the ceiling. She counted the silky loops of the fringe until she lost count.

'Clea, for God's sake,' Ben muttered, kicking the door.

She hoped he had hurt his toe. From the rough sound he made immediately afterwards she suspected he had and was pleased.

'Damn you, stay there, then,' he said, and went away.

Clea meant to. She would stay there until she turned into a skeleton if she had to.

He came back an hour later. 'I've put your salad in the fridge. There's some cold chicken with it. When you're hungry come and get it.' He was casual about it now, his temper having subsided or his mind having decided to pretend it had.

Clea didn't bother to reply. She had now counted the whole of the fringe. It had sixty-eight loops of silvery silk. She had started counting the spots on the curtains now and Ben had made her lose count. Frowning, she started off again from the beginning.

She could hear Ben breathing. He wasn't saying anything, but his tiny movements sounded so loud she could almost see him. He was trying to hear what she was doing, his hair brushing against the door panels.

'Have you been asleep?' he asked. 'Would you like some books to read? I've got a pile of them in the sitting-room. Shall I bring them for you?'

Clea concentrated on the spots. She had reached thirty-two when he started to speak again. She sighed and went back to one.

Ben said something she ignored. 'You stupid bloody little bitch,' he added, his voice shaking with temper. 'Come out of there before I smash this door down!'

Clea's concentration didn't even falter this time. She went on silently counting, her breathing so light it barely stirred the air.

'Clea,' Ben said closer to the door, a faint stirring of panic in his voice now. 'For God's sake, Clea, stop this! Say something! What are you doing in there?' He stopped. 'Clea?' he asked, anxiety naked in his voice. 'Clea!' The last was shouted.

She knew he had tried to catch sight of her through the keyhole, but she had already blocked it up with a twist of paper tissue sealed in by a strip of sticking plaster. Ben tried to pick it out with a pen but only succeeded in making a hole in the plaster, and he couldn't see much through that.

'All right,' he shouted, 'stay there until you're ready to come out.' Clea heard him stamping away down the corridor. The door slammed and she relaxed. She closed her eyes again and drifted into a semi-sleep which was comforting. Her panic had lifted from her now. She was keeping Ben at bay. All she had to do was stay obstinate, refuse to let him near her. It was only his nearness which undermined her. When he wasn't with her, her mind was cool and calm and certain. It infuriated her to know that Ben only had to start touching her for her common sense to melt like snow in summer.

Suddenly she heard voices, and shot off the bed, listening with her ear against the door. That was Natalie's voice she recognised. As she shakily started to draw back the bolt the voices stopped and she heard the slam of the front door.

Clea pulled back her own door and looked out. The flat was still. 'Natalie!' She ran to the front door and tried to open it, but it didn't move. Clea sobbed, struggling with it, waiting for Ben to appear behind her, but he didn't come. She beat with her fists on the door, shouting at the top of her voice for a moment, then stopped, tears running down her face, and stood there feeling sick and miserable.

When the tears had stopped she went back to the bedroom and washed her face. She felt oddly lightheaded and realised she was hungry again. Going into the kitchen, she hesitated, then crossly opened the fridge and got out the plate Ben had put into it, covered with a sheet of plastic wrapping.

The meal made her feel better. She drank some

tea afterwards and sat watching the round white face of the electric kitchen clock as it busily ticked round. It was nearly five o'clock, she realised. She must have slept on and off for hours.

The telephone rang in the sitting-room, and Clea rushed to it, shaking. 'Hallo? Hallo? Listen, you've got to help me ...' she began.

The phone clicked and she stared at it helplessly. 'Listen,' she began again, but it had begun to whirr and she knew whoever was on the other end had hung up. She flung it down and then stopped, staring at it. She could ring someone and ask them to get the police. Why hadn't she thought of that before?

Even as she thought of it, she heard the front door open. She stiffened, facing the open sitting-room door. Ben strolled into the room and Clea's heart sank.

The grey eyes laughed at her, a teasing amusement in them. 'Eaten your salad?'

'Was that you on the phone?'

'Of course,' he said. 'I rang from downstairs.'

Rage burned inside her as she saw the bright satisfaction in his face. He was so damned pleased with himself for having lured her out of the bedroom, got her to eat the meal. She should have known he was up to something. She knew him well enough by now to realise that he was prepared to win by any means he had to employ. He drew the line at nothing. He had no scruples where his pleasure was concerned. All he thought about was achieving the satisfaction he wanted from her.

'I despise you,' Clea said painfully, her throat hurting. 'You're completely beneath contempt! I wish Kerasteri had broken your neck instead of just knocking you out. If he was here now, that's what he would do. He'd kill you if he knew what you've been trying to force me to do.'

Ben listened grimly, his shoulders back, his face hardening, and she stopped, realising too late that she had made a mistake in mentioning her stepfather's name. For some reason it was a red rag to a bull. Ben stared at her, his eyes narrowed in cold anger.

'You wish he was here, do you? Well, he isn't, and if he was I'd knock his teeth down his throat if he tried to keep me away from you!'

'You could try,' Clea said defiantly, only to wish at once that she hadn't risked his rage. He was across the room in a flash, pulling her into his arms with a savage jerk which took her off balance.

She lifted her head to protest and his mouth crushed down on her own, silencing her muted cry. She fought to get away, her outrage muffled by that bruising pressure on her mouth, but Ben caught her head in his hands and the kiss altered to a seductive, coaxing sweetness which made her head swim. Hating herself, she tried not to yield to it, but her lips were trembling, returning the movements of his without her being able to do anything about it.

Ben groaned as he lifted his head. His eyes held that passionate, pleading intensity that made her heart sink within her as though she were in a lift.

'Darling, do you want to drive me crazy? Stop playing games. You're just wasting time we could spend far more enjoyable.' His face burrowed into her neck and he whispered at her ear, 'Clea, I need you. Don't you know what I'm going through? I can't think of anything else. You've become an obsession with me—I feel like someone on a rack.'

Clea gave a shuddering gesture of silent refusal. She had to make an enormous effort even to do that. She felt like someone holding on to a clifftop with her fingernails and knowing that a great abyss lies beneath her. If she slackened her resistance for an instant she would fall and fall until she was broken in a thousand pieces.

'You obstinate little fool!' Ben burst out, shaking her, holding her away from him to stare at her. 'Are you trying to goad me into taking you by force? Do you think I want to do it that way? What are you trying to do to me?'

'Let me go!' Clea exclaimed, meeting his angry eyes and not flinching. 'Let me leave this flat, Ben.'

'No,' he said hoarsely. 'I know you want me, and I won't let you go until you've admitted it.'

'I never will,' she said, swallowing hard.

His hard, fierce smile denied that although he said nothing.

'I'll never change my mind,' Clea insisted.

'You want me,' said Ben, with a sullen obstinacy which made him look oddly like a little boy. 'Maybe you don't even know you want me.'

'You don't even talk the same language as me,' Clea retorted with a bitter irony.

He stared at her, his brows dark. 'What?'

'You deny me the right to think for myself, act for myself, choose for myself. That's contempt. You say you love me, but you don't know what love is. If you did, you'd let me decide for myself whether I wanted to go to bed with you or not. You talk about liberation when what you mean is that the pill makes women available where they weren't before. You don't believe a woman is your equal. You wouldn't dream of telling

a man you knew better than he did what he wanted—
you know he'd punch you in the jaw if you did.'

Ben's eyes flickered as she talked in that quick, angry
voice. He was frowning, the set of his mouth impatient,
and Clea doubted if he was really listening to a word
she said.

'You haven't given me one valid reason for refusing,'
he said when she stopped talking with a weary gesture.

'I don't have to give you any reasons. I'm just saying no. Can't you get that through your head?'

'But you want me,' he insisted, his eyes glittering in
aroused excitement. 'Clea, you haven't denied that,
have you? Because you can't.'

She wished she could deny it, but her own honesty
wouldn't let her. She met his piercing stare, her face
stubborn, the calm lines of eyes, nose, mouth stiff with
determination.

Ben watched her, his face violent. 'I don't know how
you manage to make me feel like this,' he said with
husky bitterness. 'You're driving me insane. Every time
I see that obstinate, set little mouth I want to kiss it
unil you give in to me. I'm warning you—my patience
is rapidly wearing thin. If you don't listen to reason
soon I'll take you, whatever you say.'

'If you do, I'll loathe you,' said Clea, trying to make
her voice sound steady.

Ben swore under his breath and strode away from
her, slamming the door behind him.

CHAPTER EIGHT

SHE went back to the bedroom and bolted herself into it again, but now she couldn't relax, her mind so disturbed by the argument she had had with Ben that she twisted uneasily on the bed, watching the light as it roamed around the room. The afternoon was wearing slowly into a warm dusk. Clea felt isolated, as though the double-glazing locked her into a strange silent shell from which she began to feel she would never escape. Beyond it, London stretched for miles, a lonely, alien city which bore no resemblance to her own city of Athens. How many other human beings lay alone in silent rooms and watched the London skyline feeling that they were on some urban desert island?

She closed her eyes and tried to think herself back into Athens. She conjured up the hot scent of the streets in summer, the blue skies, the brilliant blinding light which gave the stark landscape such unforgettable beauty. It was only a few days away in time and only a thousand miles in space, yet she felt as though it was another planet.

Too much had happened since she left the villa for the last time. Some chemical process had been at work on her blood, and she felt her cells dissolving in the emotions Ben had set revolving inside her.

If Ben gave her another opportunity to get to the phone she could ring the police. She should have done so at once. She wished she had thought of it immediately, but her mind hadn't been working properly.

Even if he did give her a chance to use the phone, she thought with a weary realisation, would she use it?

The struggle between them was turning into a bitter duel which she felt she had to win. She did not believe Ben would use force; the idea was too unbearable. He would try to persuade her, seduce her, coax her into giving way to him. If he could do that he would have won and she would have lost. And far more turned on that duel than merely the question of whether or not she slept with him. Her own self-respect hung on it, her claim to a personal dignity as a woman.

She had left her home, her family and friends, to stake that claim for a personal dignity. If Ben really loved her he wouldn't talk to her as though she was a hypocritical, empty-headed idiot who was only waiting for him to make her give in to him, so that she could later claim she wasn't to blame for what happened.

It was entirely because she was determined to be responsible for what she did that Clea had left Greece. Ben was refusing to understand that.

While she was lying there, absorbed in thought, the light had thickened and daylight had almost gone. The street lights came on far below, their reflection gleaming through the dusk. A fine rain started, flung against the windows by a rustling wind. Clea watched it streak the glass and sighed, her body shaken with anxiety.

'Clea.' Ben tapped on the door.

'Yes?' she said, stirring, forgetting that she had not meant to answer him.

'Hungry?'

She closed her eyes. 'No.'

'You wouldn't like a light meal? Scrambled eggs? An omelette? Something easy?'

He sounded so calm and reasonable. She looked at the door and wished he would stay like that, but she knew this mood would dissolve into that fierce, passionate assault on her if she opened the door.

'No.'

Ben didn't say anything. His footsteps retreated and Clea listened to them miserably. She was tired of her own company, sick of this little room, the orange glow of the street lights through the blurring rain. A stab of homesickness made her turn on to her face, tears under her closed lids. It was cold here. She longed for the sun, the sound of cicadas and the whisper of the sea.

She wished Ben would come back; she wanted to hear his voice, even if she didn't answer him. He was another human being, although he was responsible for her isolation and loneliness.

Shivering, she got off the bed and began to undress. She might as well go to bed. She slid into her thick silk nightdress and drew the curtains to shut out that lonely, rainy night. The lamp beside the bed shed a yellow gleam over the room, and Clea lay in the bed and traced the pattern of shadows outside the rim of light.

Ben's footsteps caught her attention again. They halted outside her door and her heart raced away like a frantic animal inside her chest.

He didn't speak for a moment, his breathing low. She could feel him hesitating.

'Clea,' he whispered. 'Clea, are you asleep?'

She closed her eyes and didn't answer. She heard him touch the door, not violently, his hand brushing over the panels in a strange movement, as though he were silently pleading with her.

'Clea,' he said again in a low, tormented whisper.

She was trembling violently, huddled under the quilt, her hands clutching at it. The wind blew rain against the window. She heard it with a start, as though it was a loud noise, but it was very soft.

Ben's footsteps slowly moved away again and she relaxed her shivering body. She was drifting into sleep when she heard the sound of the front door, and jerking awake, she listened. There was no sound of voices. Had someone come in? Or gone out?

Softly she slid out of the bed and went to her door, listening with her head against it. Had Ben gone out because he thought she was asleep?

She drew back the bolt and looked out. He had caught her off guard before, she wasn't going to let him do that to her again. But if he had gone out? She might miss a chance of escape by being reluctant to take a risk.

She glanced into the next room. It was dark and empty, and by the light from the hall she realised it was another bedroom. Ben's? She moved away and began to search the flat for him.

There was no sign of him in any of the other rooms. Hurriedly, Clea ran back to the bedroom and began to strip off her nightgown. She had no time to look for clothes in her case, so she snatched up her jeans, but a sound made her spin, her face going white, her heart hammering against her throat.

Ben stood in the door staring at her, his eyes eating her as they slid down her pale naked body.

There was a second of sheer panic. She couldn't even move, held paralysed by the hunger in his stare.

Then she grabbed for the quilt with a trembling hand. Ben closed the door and bolted it.

'No!' Clea moaned.

'You're so beautiful,' Ben said unsteadily. He watched her wrap herself in the quilt without trying to stop her. 'Ever since the night I saw you at that window I've been waiting like a man possessed to see you like that again.'

She faced him, shivering inside the heavy folds of quilt. 'Where were you?'

'In my bedroom.'

'The front door clicked,' she said, hoarsely, frowning.

'Natalie going out,' Ben explained. 'She brought us some food. I asked her to keep us supplied so that I didn't have to go out.'

'You planned for me to think you'd gone out,' she accused.

'I'd do anything to get you,' he said, the shrug of his shoulders graceful and impatient. 'Can't you understand that?'

'Even to skulking about in dark rooms like a criminal?' Clea sounded contemptuous, but Ben's frown shrugged her anger away too.

'What does any of that matter? You're under my skin, in my blood, like a germ that's destroying me, Clea. I shan't be able to sleep at night until I've got you in my arms, in my bed.' His voice had roughened and deepened as he spoke and by the time he had stopped talking he was undoing his shirt, his hand trembling.

'Ben, if you come a step nearer me I'll hate you for

the rest of my life,' Clea threatened, backing in an ungainly way with the thick bulky quilt hugged round her, her hand holding it tightly.

He dropped his shirt to the floor, laughing harshly. 'We'll see about that afterwards.'

She scrambled on to the bed to get away, hampered by her own refusal to let go of her shielding quilt.

'I'm not chasing you round this room like a Marx Brothers film, Clea, so stop being stupid and give in,' said Ben, watching her. The hard flushed face was alight with a passion which terrified her. His grey eyes were moving over her all the time and his hands were clenching at his sides, but he wasn't moving towards her. Clea felt a sick resemblance of hope. Ben was in here with her and he was threatening to force her, but she still couldn't believe he would do it. He sounded insistent, but he was visibly hesitating.

She faced him across the bed like a squaw in a blanket, her head rising defiantly out of the folds of cloth.

'If you loved me, Ben, you wouldn't even consider doing this.'

'I love you, damn you,' he muttered, and still he didn't move, although his forehead bore faint traces of perspiration.

'How can you say that?'

'It's true,' he said, grimacing. 'Clea, I love you. Darling, let me prove it to you. Can't you see I'm dying for you?' He took a step and Clea backed again, shaking. Ben's grey eyes were fixed on her face, an angry pleading in them. 'I don't want to make you, but I know this is what we both want if only you would admit it.'

Her free hand fumbled behind her, searching for

some weapon she could use. The only thing she found was a small glass vase which had held some pansies, and her fingers closed round it. She threw it at Ben, who ducked. It crashed into the wall and splintered, and Ben swore. Clea was climbing back over the bed and scrambling for the door by the time he had straightened and turned. He caught her before she had unbolted the door.

'Ben!' Clea sobbed in a dry whisper.

The quilt was tugged out of her hand and thrown to one side, and Ben's devouring stare moved over her. On a helpless reflex, stricken by the expression on his face, she buried her face in his shoulder, curving her body into his to hide her nakedness. Ben took a long, deep intake of air and his arms went round her.

His warm skin lay under her cheek and she heard the deep hurried beat of his heart against her naked breasts. He ran his hand down her curved body, following the line of the spine with a possessive, exploring touch. Her pulses clamoured like fire against her neck and wrists. She remembered the night she had stood at that window and been fixed for a shaken moment with Ben's eyes moving over her white body. If she was honest with herself this had been in both their minds at that moment. Clea had known as she looked at herself in the mirror a few moments later that her whole nerve system was jangling with desire.

Ben turned his dark head to bury his lips at the side of her neck. 'Oh, Clea, at last! I've wanted you so much since that night.'

It was in his mind, too. They had both known as they stared at each other in that fevered silence.

Passivity held her like a drug, all her ability to think

sealed away. The movements of his hands and mouth were making her senses go crazy. The glass shell which had held her ever since she was brought to this flat had closed in on her now, trapping her, and the emotions eating at her were depriving her of the strength to fight him any longer.

Ben put a hand under her chin and firmly turned her head towards him. She looked up, trembling. The grey eyes were alight with need and desire. Without a word Ben bent his head and she yielded her lips with a childlike submission.

The kiss broke from seductive coaxing into flame, the pressure of his mouth sending her head back. She clung to him, giving her mouth without resistance.

Ben broke off the kiss with a smothered groan of pleasure, to look down at her again. His hands slid down her smooth body and lifted her triumphantly. Clea's heart was hurting as it raced inside her. As Ben carried her to the bed she struggled like someone drowning to wake up before it was too late.

Ben deposited her gently on the bed, kneeling on it, his hand going out to switch off the lamp. Clea slid off the other side and he lifted his head, surprised by the movement.

'Don't start that again, Clea,' he said harshly.

'I can't let you do it to me,' she told him in a thin high voice. 'I can't, Ben. I won't!'

'For God's sake,' he bit out, a savage darkness coming into his eyes, 'do you want to send me insane? We've been through all this over and over again. Just now there was no shadow of doubt anywhere, was there? You were wanting me as much as I wanted you. Stop playing games—I've lost patience with you!'

'I'm not playing games,' Clea denied, frightened by the anger in his eyes and voice but refusing to let him browbeat her into submission. 'I refuse to go to bed with you and I don't think you'll make me, Ben.'

'Don't be so damned sure,' Ben grated, dark red colour flowing up his face. He stared at her, his teeth set. 'I'll give you one more chance to give up this ridiculous pretence of reluctance, then I'm taking what you seem determined to force me to take.'

'If you do, I'll hate you!' Clea backed until she was against the wall, her lip caught between her teeth.

Ben walked round the bed, his hard face set. 'Hate me, then,' he muttered as he yanked her away from the wall and threw her roughly back on to the bed. Before Clea could scramble off it again he was beside her. The light went out and she was blind, helpless, Ben's thigh trapping her under him, his hands sliding over her trembling body.

'There's a very unpleasant word for women like you,' he ground out through his teeth. 'You've been teasing me ever since we met, driving me crazy without meaning to give me what your eyes have promised me every time I kissed you. If you honestly didn't want me you would have made that very clear by now. But although you protest and push me away you make damned sure you keep me running after you, don't you? Your body convicts you every time I touch it.'

She saw the glitter of his eyes in the dark, felt his hand closing over her breast. 'Oh, no!' she moaned, trying to fight the sensation of intense pleasure taking over her.

'Oh, yes,' Ben mocked, and buried his hot face between her breasts, his thigh trembling against her. 'My

God, I want you, Clea. Tell me you want me, too.'

She was too busy trying to stop the rush of blood singing in her ears, the shaking of her body as Ben's mouth moved against it. Her hair had been flung across her eyes and she couldn't get a hand free to brush it away. Blinded by it, she struggled to stop Ben parting her thighs and in the end he grew angry, using a ruthless force to make her yield to him.

She tensed, writhing under him, the brush of his body sending shivers down her back. 'Don't!' she gasped, and Ben's mouth stopped the hoarse cry. There was a muffled cry of pain from her a second later, but it didn't halt Ben's invasion. Clea involuntarily lifted her arms to push him away and as he moved again her fingers dug into his bare shoulders. He didn't seem to notice that, either. He was kissing her hungrily, his body driving with a relentless force which she had no chance of escaping. A scalding rush of tears escaped from her closed eyes. Ben felt them against his face and lifted his head with a muttered swear word.

'Damn you, don't!' he exploded, staring down at her pale face in the darkness.

'You're hurting me!'

He lay still. 'I'm sorry.' There was a faintly sulky sound to that. 'I didn't mean to. God, Clea, you made me so angry!'

'You hurt me,' she said again, the tears running down her face.

'Don't cry,' he whispered, kissing the wet side of her cheek. 'Oh, hell, Clea, don't. I don't want to hurt you. I just want to love you.'

'*Love* me?' she sobbed, almost laughing in her anger.

He kissed her lingeringly, his lips warm and gentle.

'Clea, Clea, darling,' he said against her mouth, 'I want you so badly.'

She lay there, trembling, her mouth parted and yielding to his kisses. Ben stroked her softly like some one gentling a frightened animal, his hand moving from breast to thigh, sending little ripples of enjoyment along her skin.

'You're so lovely,' he told her, a sigh in his voice. 'Stop fighting me, darling.'

Clea listened without moving, the comforting brush of his hand half sending her to sleep. When he parted her mouth with his own she made no attempt to reject him; she found the coaxing exploration of his kiss too pleasurable. It deepened gradually into a demanding passion and she gave it back, her body supple and yielding in his hands.

'Oh, Clea,' he gasped, his body taut again abruptly as though her response had spun him back into that blinding core of desire.

Clea tried not to be dragged with him down into that pulsating flame, but she had given way too far to her own passion. Her arms went round his neck, clinging. Her body trembled and vibrated under him. Eyes closed, she passed through barrier after barrier of pleasure, the revolving circles of piercing excitement quickening, the thrust of his body driving them both beyond any ability to control their reactions until their mutual cries of agonised satisfaction had died away.

Clea lay with eyes closed, shuddering, and Ben lay beside her breathing so roughly he seemed to be snatching at air like a drowning man. The room was intensely quiet.

I wish I were dead, Clea thought.

As her passion died away so a melancholy crept inside her, colouring the way she saw what had just happened, making her feel that she had betrayed herself in giving way to Ben. She put her arm over her eyes and felt wetness stealing out from under her lids.

Ben shifted to touch his mouth to her bare shoulder. 'I thought I'd die,' he said, a lazy smile in his voice. 'Fantastic, wasn't it, darling?' He stroked her breast gently. Clea tensed, not answering. 'Once you stopped being afraid you realised I was right, didn't you?' Ben asked. 'It was what you wanted too.'

She was admitting that to herself already. She had admitted it inside her head long ago. It made no difference to her refusal. The fact that she found Ben sexually attractive was beside the point; she found him too many other things as well. Ben had not just been trying to make her admit she wanted him. He believed that she had just proved to him that all women were available if you were persistent enough, determined enough. He had taken her with contempt, refusing to let her make up her own mind. She would never forgive him for that. In overriding her opposition Ben had made her feel as contemptible as he thought she was. He had made her match the image of a woman which he carried around in his head. Clea found that unforgivable.

'You're very quiet,' Ben murmured. 'Still surprised to find you enjoyed it?' He laughed as he said that. She heard the laughter and hated him.

He waited for her to reply and when she didn't he pulled her arm down and leaned up on one elbow to look into her face, frowning as he saw the tearstains. 'Oh, hell, you're not crying again?' He sighed and then gave her a quick, coaxing smile. 'You're not going to dissolve into tears every time we go to bed, I hope.' He was trying to make her laugh, trying to charm her into good humour. His own humour was dancing in the grey eyes. He was still elated, triumphant, very high on the drug of satisfaction he had just snatched from her.

She didn't say a word, looking at him with blank, dull eyes. Self-disgust and anger had not yet shattered the listless misery holding her. The end-of-passion melancholy wrapped her round.

'What's the matter now?' Ben demanded, impatience in his face. 'My God, Clea, you can be infuriating! Don't try to kid me that you didn't enjoy it as much as I did—I know damn well you did. I knew you would. Didn't I keep telling you that all you had to do was stop protesting? I know it hurt a bit, it always does the first time and I was a bit rough with you—I'm sorry. Believe me, I didn't mean to be, but you made me angry. It was fantastic later, though, wasn't it?'

She shifted her eyes and her body shuddered in a painful sigh.

'Don't ignore me,' Ben erupted, pulling her head round again. 'I'm talking to you. Answer me!'

She silently shook her head.

He stared at her, the smile going out of his eyes, his cheekbones hardening. 'I see. That's the treatment I'm going to get now, is it?'

He was off the bed a second later, snatching up his clothes. She didn't watch him as he rapidly dressed, but she heard the angry pace of his movements. She didn't care. Her body was slack and exhausted, her mind in a very similar state.

Ben swivelled to look at her. She didn't look at him, but she felt the brooding impatience of his stare.

'Sulk if you want to, but let's have a little damned honesty around here. Is it because we aren't married? You had your chance to get married and be respectably free to go to bed with a man, but you turned it down, and quite rightly. You didn't want him and you weren't prepared to take marriage if you had to take him too. But you do want me. I just haven't given you a ring and a little bit of paper which says it's legal. That's what this is all about, really, isn't it?'

Clea looked at him then, her face twisting with bitter irony. 'You wouldn't even begin to understand if I told you.'

'Try me!'

'I've tried. You and I can't communicate.'

'We just did,' Ben said, his voice deepening. 'Beautifully.'

She bit her lip and looked away.

'Who needs language if they can communicate like that?' He was softening again, laughing.

'That wasn't communication, it was lust.'

Ben swore savagely. 'That's a lie! I had to make you admit the truth about yourself and there was only one way I could do that.' He moved away and opened the door. 'Clea, once you've got over the first shock you'll realise you've been making a fuss over nothing.'

'Go away,' Clea burst out, looking at him bitterly. 'I wish I'd never left Athens!'

Ben stiffened. 'I knew that was at the back of your mind! You're afraid of what Kerasteri will think when he hears you're living with me, aren't you? I can tell you what he'll think—he'll go crazy with jealousy. But there's nothing he can do about it.' He laughed, his face dark red with anger. 'You belong to me now, and I'm keeping you. Kerasteri can eat his heart out!'

The door slammed, and Clea heard him stride away. She winced, feeling sick. How much of Ben's determination to make her give way to him came from a peculiar twisted hatred of her stepfather? Every time she mentioned Kerasteri, Ben became violent. Her stepfather had treated him with kindly contempt from that first meeting when Melissa brought Ben to the villa. Ben was too quick not to have picked it up. And he was too egotistical to have enjoyed knowing that the other man regarded him as some sort of lesser being.

Clea wondered if she had become some sort of trophy to Ben, the prize he had snatched from Kerasteri. Ben was oddly ambivalent about his Greek blood. He never mentioned his mother. She could understand why. Ben's contempt for women came from what he had learnt of them from his mother at an early age. The fact that Kerasteri was Greek and that he seemed to Ben to be possessive about Clea might well have triggered off Ben's tenacity in pursuing her. He might not even realise how far he was motivated by a subconscious desire for revenge on women when he treated them with that mocking contempt.

She knew she wasn't going to sleep. The quiet night hours ticked past. Occasionally she heard a movement, a whisper of music, from the sitting-room and she knew Ben was awake, too. It was only towards dawn that she realised what he was doing. She heard his stumbling footsteps coming towards the door, heard his bedroom door crash and a muffled curse as he tripped over something.

Ben was drunk, she recognised. For a few moments he moved around the other bedroom, then she heard the bedsprings give. After a while the silence settled back over the flat.

Clea got up and showered quietly. She dressed and got her case. There wasn't a sound from Ben. She went down the hall and tried the door. It was still locked. She put down her case and crept back to Ben's door. It creaked as she slid it open. The room was grey with beginning light, and Clea looked quickly at the bed. Ben's black head was turned away from her. He was sleeping heavily, his skin hot.

His clothes lay scattered across the floor. She began to look through his pockets, her hands trembling.

She found a key-ring after a moment and straightened, stealing a look at Ben. He hadn't moved. There was a quality about his sleep which made her sure he wouldn't wake up; he was fathoms deep in drunken stupor.

She tried four keys before one fitted. Carrying her case, she made her way down the stairs. The front door of the house was locked too. Clea found another key which fitted that lock. She left the key in the door when she closed it, so Ben would find it when he woke up.

London still slept, the grey streets empty except for an occasional early milkman, his electric motor whining as he made his rounds. Clea had no idea where she was going or even where she was, except that it was Knightsbridge. At the moment that didn't seem to matter. All that mattered was that she was getting away from Ben and the whole miserable episode which had left her feeling betrayed and sick.

CHAPTER NINE

SHE got a job quite easily. The first agency she contacted were able to fix her up with a post as a receptionist at a large London hotel. Clea pointed out anxiously that she had no qualifications, but the girl at the agency just laughed. 'Take a look in a mirror,' she advised.

Startled, Clea asked: 'What?'

'You're easy on the eye and you've got a pleasant smile,' the girl told her. 'That's all the qualifications you're going to need.'

When Clea saw the hotel manager he was equally reassuring. 'Our receptionist walked out without a moment's notice,' he groaned. 'I'm desperate—it isn't easy to get good staff. I need someone polite and nice-looking who can keep her temper and make our guests feel she's really interested in their problems. You don't need any other qualification.'

'I speak a little French,' Clea offered shyly. 'And, of course, fluent Greek.'

'Great,' he said, laughing. 'But we've got an interpreter, so if you run into any language problems you just give him a shout. I hope you'll stay with us, Clea, at least until the worst of the season is over. I'm sick of staff who walk out without warning.'

It took Clea several weeks to adjust to her new pattern of living. She wasn't used to the routine of a working life, getting up at a certain time each day, being more or less chained to the reception desk during working hours. But her nature disposed her to work hard and she soon found her feet in the job. The staff were always changing, people came and went all the time. There was a temporary feel to the place which was not confined to the guests.

'We have to take what we can get,' the manager told her, making a wry face. 'People drop in and work for us for a few weeks, then shove off again. That's the sort of business it is, I'm afraid.'

Clea had been given a staff room in the hotel because it was so hard to find a flat in London. Working with people all day one got quite friendly with them, but Clea couldn't feel that she belonged there. She too, felt temporary.

She spent most of her free time alone, exploring London or walking in the nearby park, her mind occupied with thoughts she found painful. She had written a brief, regretful letter to Kerasteri once she had got the job at the hotel. She tried to explain to him her reasons for leaving, guessing that her stepfather would not understand or be ready to forgive her, but it did not surprise her when she got no reply. Kerasteri would feel that she had betrayed him by walking out on her arranged marriage.

Being alone so much she found plenty of time to think about her relationship with her stepfather. Ben's accusations had horrified her so much in the beginning that she had never even paused to wonder how much truth there was in them. On her own side, none at all. She had never thought of Kerasteri as anything but her stepfather. But she wasn't quite so certain about his feelings. Looking back over the past couple of years she realised that his warmly demonstrative feelings towards her could have been misinterpreted by a stranger. Kerasteri didn't hesitate to kiss her, stroke her cheek, walk with an arm around her waist—all the actions of a lover in one context. What Ben could not understand had seemed quite normal to Clea, used to her stepfather's hugs and kisses since childhood. If there had been any extra dimension to Kerasteri's feelings, Clea preferred not to think about it. He had never given her any reason to suspect such a thing and she refused to believe it.

A few weeks after she started work she did get a letter from Melissa, a short hurriedly written little note, half complaining, half envying her. Melissa wrote that Kerasteri was too angry even to speak about her at the moment. 'Maybe one day he'll forgive you,' Melissa said without much hope. She added a PS: Write to me, but don't expect me to write back too often. You know I hate writing letters. But keep in touch.

Clea got the distinct impression that Melissa had written without her father's approval or even perhaps his knowledge. Melissa wasn't the sort of girl to be prepared to risk a quarrel with her father except over something she wanted badly. She always did in secret what she knew he would dislike. Clea wondered as she finished reading the letter how Melissa could bear to live like that, always hiding her thoughts, her feelings, her actions. Life for her was a constant battle of wits.

Clea often felt isolated in London's crowded, lonely streets, but at least she had the self-respect of knowing that she had chosen her own path. Freedom was a lonely condition, perhaps, yet it was the only one Clea was prepared to accept. Melissa's life was going to be a series of compromises, deceits, petty betrayals; Clea would not live like that.

One lunchtime she took her sandwiches out into the nearby park. Autumn sunlight was shafting over the lawns. In the distance a lake shone with a blue brightness which reminded her of Greece and brought on the nostalgia for shadowed pines and blue water which was becoming a recurrent motif in her life. She knew she would never go back to Greece to live, but she missed the beauty of the landscape and the explosive nature of the Greek way of life.

She missed Kerasteri, she missed Melissa; they had been so deep a part of her life. Watching leaves blowing in a windy dance across the grass to build up in drifts of brown and amber under the hedges, Clea sighed. One had to pay for everything. Soon the leaves would all have gone. The trees would be bare, their present blaze of colour stripped away. That was how she felt. She had been left emotionally bare, first by leaving her home and the only family she knew, and then by Ben's violent possession of her.

A child was playing with a dog nearby, and Clea watched, envying him. His face was alight with the sheer joy of being alive. But Clea felt no joy in life at all. She felt null and empty.

She had not been happy since she faced the fact that she had to leave Greece; and Ben had broken something inside her when he forced her. It wasn't the physical surrender which had damaged her. It was the emotional surrender. Ben had been possessing her physically, but she had been giving herself without reserve, body, mind and heart. The exchange had been unequal; she had always known it would be—that was

why she had refused to let him make love to her. Ben
would not understand if she explained to him. Love
was entirely physical to him.

Sometimes she wondered if he actually hated women.
It would explain his dark insistence, his tenacious
pursuit, so that the moment when he forced them to
surrender to him was an act of destruction, of revenge.

She shook free of her thoughts. She had promised
herself to stop thinking about Ben. The best thing she
could do was to forget him. Until she did she would
never achieve any peace of mind.

She ate her sandwiches and threw the crusts to the
pigeons before walking back to the hotel. She could
eat in the dining-room, but she preferred to have a
break from the hotel now and then.

The other receptionist was on duty at the desk, dealing with a Japanese couple whose English wasn't adequate to the problem of explaining that they wanted a
quieter room. The people in the next room made too
much noise, they appeared to be saying, but their vo-
cabulary kept deserting them and they would search
their little phrase book for a way of describing their
obvious fury, pointing at words with impatient little
jabs of a finger.

As Clea appeared, the girl sighed with relief. 'My
colleague will help you,' she said, smiling politely at
the Japanese couple.

'Please?' they said, looking at Clea.

The other girl slid away, winking at Clea, who gave
all her attention to working out what the jerky phrases
culled from the little book meant and finally understood. She arranged for them to be moved at once
and, smiling, they rushed off to photograph London.

'Had a good lunch?' the other girl asked, joining her again now that the problem had been satisfactorily resolved.

'Sandwiches in the park.' Clea straightened the desk diary and lifted the phone as it began to shrill.

'I'm going to a disco tonight with Bob,' the other girl said. 'What are you doing?'

Clea shrugged. 'I haven't decided.'

'Why don't you come? You might meet someone.'

Clea smiled briefly. 'Thanks, but I'm not in the mood.' She did not want to meet anyone. The last thing she wanted was to meet anyone.

A couple had come through the swing doors and were talking to the hall porter. Clea idly glanced at them and got a shock as she recognised Natalie. Natalie hadn't looked her way yet, so Clea shot behind the desk and vanished into the filing room at the back of it. She made a pretence of consulting the steel cabinets for several moments. When she warily looked out the foyer was empty and Natalie had gone.

For a few days after starting work here, Clea had been afraid that Ben would somehow find out where she was and appear at the hotel, but as the days went by and there was no sign of him she had stopped worrying about it. Now she felt very nervous as she handled guests checking in and out. She kept looking across the foyer, half dreading the sight of Ben walking into the hotel.

She was sure Natalie hadn't noticed her, but her mind couldn't stay on what she was doing. Her colleague looked at her in amusement. 'You're in a weird mood today. That chap asked you the way to Buckingham Palace and you told him it was across the road!'

Clea groaned. 'Did I? Poor man, he'll be surprised to find himself looking at Boots!'

'Something on your mind?' Janet asked, staring.

Clea shrugged the question away and another guest came up to distract Janet's curiosity.

For the next few days Clea felt distinctly uneasy. Every time someone walked into the hotel she shot a nervous look towards the doors before she relaxed. Janet teased her, determined to find out what was making her so tense and edgy.

'What's he like? Come on, you can tell me.'

'Tall, dark and handsome,' Clea said drily.

'No, honestly!' Janet laughed.

'He is,' Clea insisted with a sense of irony. It was as good a description of Ben as she could imagine, but it left out so much of the reality of him.

One morning an elderly lady with a discontented, irritable face marched up to the desk as Janet and Clea were talking and tapped with an impatient hand. 'Would one of you mind serving me, or is that too much to ask?'

'Yours, Janet,' Clea said under her breath.

Janet went forward with her bright smile and Clea leaned on the counter and stared at the clock, waiting for her lunch break. She wasn't hungry. Her appetite since she came to London had been very poor. She was eager, though, to get out of the hotel and into the autumn sunshine.

They were having a sort of Indian summer, everyone told her. It wasn't always like this in October in England. The calm, mellow days were a rare bonus from the weatherman.

'Make the most of it,' Janet warned her. 'When it's

gone we'll be plunged into rain and gloom again.'

Clea preferred not to imagine that. She was finding London quite beautiful under blue autumn skies. With the trees stripping for winter the melancholy streets had their own appeal, walking the thin line between ugliness and beauty and often depending on the mood of the beholder.

Every day Clea walked to the nearest London park. The lawns were littered with withering leaves, there were people sitting on the benches feeding the pigeons who strutted and begged for crumbs, the borders of the flower beds were alive with smoky-scented, smoky-coloured chrysanthemums.

Today as she wandered along the paths the air had a crisp cool tang to it as though winter were getting nearer, but the sun still danced on the lake and people still sat about with their faces turned contentedly to the sky.

Clea found a spare bench and sat down, and at once the pigeons flocked around her, their wings displayed as they fluttered around her feet. She began to throw her unwanted sandwiches to them, watching them grab at the small pieces and fly off with them.

Someone stopped beside her and she looked up, a smile ready, only to have it die on her as she recognised Ben.

'Hello, Clea,' he said.

She half rose as if to escape and he sat down abruptly, his hand grabbing her wrist and anchoring her on the bench. 'No,' he said. 'We have to talk.'

'We've got nothing to say to each other.' She stared at him with hostility, angry with herself because even as she frowned she was aware that she was absorbing

every detail of how he looked. He was wearing a dark
pin-striped suit. She had never seen him look so remote and formal. At a quick glance he might have
been any of the city businessmen who came in and
out of the hotel to sit through boring business lunches
and drink and eat more than they wanted to or were
wise to, judging by their glazed faces as they staggered
out later.

'You don't look well,' Ben told her with a flat intona-
tion. He had been staring at her, too. She looked down,
knowing that her skin had lost that golden suntan
and a city pallor was beginning to creep over her
face. She hadn't slept well since she got to London. The
faint blue shadows under her eyes betrayed that to
him.

'Sorry,' Clea said bitterly. What did he expect? How
dare he say she didn't look well?

'You found a job, then,' he said.

Clea was not going to sit here making polite conversation with him as though he was a distant acquaintance who hadn't seen her for a while. She watched
the pigeons fighting over the last pieces of bread, their
round gleaming eyes vicious as they pecked each other,
and didn't say anything.

'As talkative as ever,' Ben muttered, shifting in his
place with suppressed impatience.

'I told you—I've got nothing to say to you.'

'Aren't you curious to know how I found you?'

'Natalie,' shrugged Clea. She had already guessed
that. Natalie had seen her, after all. She should have
know that Natalie was too clever to let her get any
warning; she had pretended not to notice her in order
to lull her into a false sense of security.

Ben shrugged his wide shoulders. 'Yes,' he admitted. 'So you did see her? She thought you might not have noticed her.'

'Oh, I noticed her,' Clea said icily. 'I wasn't likely to forget her.'

Ben grimaced, his hard mouth twisting. 'No.' She met his eyes and he looked away. With his face in profile he had a stark sort of beauty, the self-willed mockery of the grey eyes hidden and the strong bones of his face tight under his brown skin.

She did not want to watch him. She tried to make herself look away, but she couldn't stop feeding the unsatisfied hunger of her heart with this glimpse of him. It didn't make her feel any more kindly towards him; she was even angrier because of her own stupid weakness.

He shifted impatiently beside her, then broke out: 'Clea, how could you just disappear like that? I've been through seven different kinds of hell. I was terrified of what might have happened to you.'

Clea laughed angrily and saw him flinch.

'I'm serious. I've been desperately worried about you. I couldn't believe you'd run out on me at first.' He made a self-accusing face. 'When I woke up I had a head like a cement mixer and I felt terrible. Then I realised you'd gone and I felt much worse.'

'How sad,' Clea flung back in icy dislike.

'Don't,' he muttered, his head lowered towards the ground.

There was a silence, then he said: 'I thought you might have gone back to Greece, so I flew there to see if you had.'

Her hands locked tight in her lap, the knuckles turning white. 'Did you see Kerasteri?'

'Briefly.'

'What happened?'

'He threw me out,' Ben said drily. 'Literally. I put a foot over the threshold and he sent me flying. True, he picked me up afterwards, but that was to shake me like a terrier shaking a rat and demand to know where I'd taken you.'

'Oh, no!' exclaimed Clea.

'Your stepfather's a violent man. I thought for a minute he was going to kill me.'

'A pity he didn't!'

'Thank you.' Ben undid his jacket and pushed his hands into his pockets, the wind lifting his black hair and blowing it into a tangle.

'Did he say anything about me?' Clea asked a moment later, breaking their silence.

'Not really. Except to ask if I knew where you were. But I didn't get the impression he was very pleased with you. He seemed convinced you'd run off with me.'

Clea had expected that that was what Kerasteri would decide. It didn't surprise her to hear that he had.

'I shoved off when Melissa came shrieking out of the villa and began begging him not to get upset because he might have a heart attack. She didn't seem to mind if he killed me.'

'Why should she?'

Ben grimaced. 'All right, I deserve that. But I've been looking for you non-stop ever since you ran off. I had a private detective searching London. God knows how he came to miss you. I suggested he toured the hotels first—I remembered you'd talked of being a receptionist.'

'Well, you can set your mind at rest,' she said with

icy bitterness. 'I've got a good job and somewhere to live and I can do without help from anyone.'

'Clea, listen to me ...'

She thrust his hand away as he moved it to touch her arm urgently. 'Keep your hands off me!'

His colour darkened. 'Can't you see how worried I've been? I've been like a madman. I even got in touch with the police and the hospitals. I had a terrifying picture of you ...' He broke off as though he couldn't quite bring himself to put that into words, but she picked up what he meant.

Looking at him with contempt, she asked: 'Did you think I'd killed myself?'

His wince told her that he had thought exactly that.

'What did you think I'd choose? The river? Or did you imagine I'd chuck myself under a train?'

'Don't, for God's sake, Clea,' he muttered, his head moving lower as though the weight of pain depressing it made it impossible to hold it up.

'I didn't get much change from any of them,' he said. 'I had no authority to ask them to look for you. They said you'd probably gone back home to your family and when my detective failed to pick up your trail, that was what I thought might have happened. So I went to Greece. When you weren't there either I thought I'd really go out of my mind.'

'I hope it kept you awake at night,' Clea said bitterly, thinking of her own sleepless nights, the times when she had turned over in the bed, shuddering at the memory of that night with him. Had he been awake, too? Had he been remembering? But the memory wouldn't be the same for him. He hadn't been torn to shreds

by a selfish, self-involved devil who despised even as
he caressed.

'If it's any comfort to you, it did,' said Ben, and the
sound of his voice held a pain which she couldn't
pretend she didn't hear.

There was silence between them for a long moment,
and Clea felt her pulses beating painfully. She wanted
to get up and walk away, but she was held there by
a peculiar, rapt absorption in pain.

People kept walking past them, sometimes glancing
towards them curiously, as though even a casual eye
could pick up the emotions eating them. Clea felt her
own well-known, familiar pain altering, growing, as
though her recognition of his pain was feeding the
feelings she had come to know so well, fertilising them,
increasing them. They both sat there staring at the
path intently, saying nothing, yet there was a constant
communication between them, like a pulse beating on
the quiet air.

She was hardly aware of where they were. One tiny
compartment of her mind retained the knowledge that
they were sitting on a park bench in London sunshine
with lawns and trees and a lake in the distance. That
part of her registered the passing people, too, without
seeing them or making any distinction between one
and another. They might have been shadows in a
dream. All that made any sense was that she was with
Ben and trapped in an intense emotion.

'I behaved like a swine,' he admitted suddenly.

'Oh, you've finally recognised that?' She didn't turn
to look at him, but her voice lashed him, eager to
draw blood.

She knew she had achieved her object. Ben moved,

restlessly, his body drawing in on itself in a recoil
from what she had said. 'Clea give me a chance to
explain.' His voice shook, although it came very
quietly, the sound of it only just audible because she
was straining to hear.

'I already understand.'

'You do?' He lifted his head and looked towards her.

'You behaved like a swine because you are a swine.'

'God!' he groaned, dropping his head again. 'I
thought if I could get you to listen to me I could make
you understand what was happening to me, but I can't
seem to find the right words.'

Words were only an expansion of what the heart
picked up without heeding them. Clea did not need
to have him tell her how he had felt, she remembered
only too well.

'I think I was demented,' Ben said slowly. 'I know
I was obsessed, acting like a madman. I had this fixed
idea that if only I could get you into bed you would
belong to me.'

'You can't own people.' That was what she had
learnt in Greece—that was why she had left. She
would not be owned or used by anyone, she was her
own property.

'You're so damned cool,' Ben broke out roughly. 'I
wanted to shatter your coolness, see you break up in
my arms.'

She had already realised that. Ben had been acting
under some sort of self-driven need to impose himself
on her. The drive for power was inherent in all human
beings. They needed to force other people to admit
their power even if it might destroy those who have
submitted. In a man it often took the form of a physi-

cal attempt to force submission. A woman, unable to use physical strengths, used other weapons which could be just as destructive.

What had made Clea so angry was not that Ben had attempted to force her to submit but that he had succeeded. The little death which overcomes a human being at the point of sexual satisfaction is not lightly named. At that moment the body stops, the heart, the brain, the lungs all briefly halted for a beat of time. Ben had destroyed Clea that night. When her heart-beat picked up again, her lungs sucking in air, her mind re-establishing awareness, she had been left with the sense of melancholy which always comes at such moments, but a sadness increased by the knowledge that she had lost something of herself to Ben for ever, without getting back an equal love.

'I've never liked women much,' Ben said drily. 'I've never trusted or respected them. I can't remember ever feeling anything but suspicion towards them. However much I enjoyed their company I couldn't help dis-counting everything they said to me. I thought they were all liars, all flirts, all cheats. I knew they loved to make men want them, enjoyed being chased. I was convinced that what they were after was to see a man on his knees just for the fun of kicking him in the teeth and walking away.'

Clea listened intently. The shadows of a sycamore moved on the path beside them and her eyes followed the shifting tracery of darkness.

'I couldn't believe you were different. I thought you just refused to admit what you were. I wanted to make you admit it.'

Ben was always attacking before he could be attacked,

always determined to force submission before he could be forced to submit himself. He had grown up on the defensive, launching himself at life with hostility, his mother's desertion leaving him with an inbred aggression towards all women that refused to trust or like them.

'At first when I realised you'd got away I was violently angry. It was only as the days went by and I couldn't find you that I realised it had become a matter of necessity to me to find you.'

'All you ever think of is yourself,' said Clea, getting up. She took him by surprise and he was too late to stop her, but he caught at her arm, his face broken up into lines of pain.

'Clea, listen. Please, you've got to listen to me!'

'I've been listening, but all you talk about is yourself. You see the whole world as a mirror whose only reason for existence is to send back reflections of yourself.'

'God!' he muttered, drawing a harsh breath. 'You don't understand ...'

'I understand you only too well. Stay away from me or I'll complain to the police that you're pestering me.'

'Clea, I love you,' he said fiercely.

'Love? You don't know the meaning of the word!'

'I didn't,' he said under his breath, his hand refusing to release her. 'I admit I didn't. But I do now.' He stopped, swallowing, then said huskily: 'Clea, marry me.'

'You bastard,' she whispered, staring at him in frozen pain.

He misunderstood. Bending towards her, he said

quickly: 'I mean it. I love you. At the back of my head I think I always knew I loved you, but I was too obsessed with my belief that women weren't to be taken seriously to realise that this time I was really in love.' He put his other hand against her cheek, his fingers shaking. 'Darling, I've been miserable since you ran out on me. I've hated myself.'

'That makes two of us, then,' Clea said with sickness in her throat. 'I wouldn't marry you to save my life. I'd rather be torn apart by wild horses than marry a man who could treat me the way you did!'

Ben stiffened, his face draining of all colour. Clea looked him up and down with a contemptuous little smile before her shook free of him and walked away.

CHAPTER TEN

A WEEK later, Clea was working at the reception desk, dealing with a man who had lost his luggage in flight and was distraught because he was convinced he would never get it back. 'I haven't even got a toothbrush,' he kept saying.

'You can buy anything you need, sir,' Clea murmured. 'But the airline has promised faithfully to locate the luggage and have it sent here as soon as they can.'

'I haven't even got a toothbrush,' he said again, running a hand through his hair until he looked like a man who had seen a ghost.

There was someone standing behind him. Clea was concentrating on the distracted face in front of her, but out of the corner of her eye she received an impression of red hair and jerked to attention, her glance flying sideways.

Natalie stared back at her. Clea looked away, her brow wrinkling. 'I'm sure the airline will do their best, sir. Don't worry. As soon as they ring us I'll let you know.'

'I haven't even got a toothbrush,' he said, walking away.

'I've got to talk to you,' said Natalie, moving up to the desk.

Clea shrugged. 'I'm sorry, I'm on duty, and we have nothing to say to each other.'

Natalie leaned over, one hand on the grained wood, her fingernails blood-coloured. 'Are you deaf? I said I've got to talk to you and I mean now.'

'I'm on duty.' Clea didn't raise her voice, but her face had a calm, immovable obstinacy.

'Get someone to take over.' Natalie glanced along the foyer at Janet who was talking to the hall porter, giggling. 'She works here, doesn't she? Ask her.'

'She's off duty,' Clea said.

'For God's sake!' Natalie turned and walked towards Janet, and Clea stared after her furiously. Who did she think she was?

Natalie spoke to Janet and Janet smiled, looking surprised and curious. They came back together.

'I'll mind the desk for you, Clea.' Janet opened the counter and gestured for Natalie to pass through in front of her. 'You can talk in the office.'

Clea was not going to argue about it in front of Janet. She silently turned and led the way into the office behind the reception area. When Natalie closed the door Clea leaned on the desk with her hands supporting her and looked at her coldly.

'Well?'

'If you're going to take that attitude we aren't going to get very far.' Natalie was bristling, her green eyes hard, resenting Clea's coolness.

'I don't know why you're here,' said Clea flatly.

'If you refuse to listen, how can I tell you?'

'I'm listening. Get it over with.'

Natalie was wearing a finely cut cream suit with a pleated, formal skirt. She moved, the pleats swirling round her long legs, impatience in the way she walked.

'Ben's sick,' she said abruptly.

'Get a doctor.'

'My God, you're hard,' Natalie muttered, staring at her. 'You know what I mean. He isn't eating, he isn' doing anything, he just shuts himself up and brood all day. He looks ill.'

'He isn't my problem.'

'But that's just it, isn't it? He is.' The red hair flamed as sunlight caught it from the window behind Clea Natalie picked up a cardboard file from the desk and looked at it without really seeing it. 'He's crazy abou you and it's driving him insane.'

'That won't last long,' Clea said. She was refusing to listen at anything but the sheer surface level of hear ing, her mind shutting off and not accepting wha Natalie was saying. She did not want to be dragged back into the torment of feeling. Since she last saw Ben she had been suppressing all memory, refusing to let herself think about him.

Natalie put down the file. 'He hasn't told me much but I know him pretty well.'

Clea looked at her sharply. 'You console him, then, she said, her voice edged with ice.

Natalie's green eyes flashed, satisfaction in them and Clea felt heat rush into her face. She was furiou with herself for that unguarded reaction. She knew that the jealousy she felt had showed in her voice.

'Look, I've never meant a thing to Ben,' Natalie said frankly. 'Oh, we had a brief fling some years back but when I realised it was all on my side I backed out I wasn't wasting my time on a man who never reall saw me.'

'Very wise,' Clea said coldly.

'Ben's always been a bit warped about women. He

can be great company and he's charming, but he's
very cynical. You see, his mother . . .'

'I know all that,' Clea interrupted.

'You do?' Natalie looked at her searchingly. 'He told
you what a rotten childhood he had? Every now and
then his mother would swoop down and make a big
fuss of him, with armfuls of expensive presents and
promises to take him to Paris or New York with her,
then she'd disappear again without warning. Ben came
to hate her. He still does.'

Clea listened, her face disturbed. 'I can understand
that.'

'So can I,' said Natalie. 'Poor old Ben! When he
grew up he realised he could pull a bird without really
trying. They just formed queues for him.' She shrugged.
'They still do. When he first talked about you, I got
the idea you were just a girl playing hard to get. I'll
admit I was surprised when I met you, but women
never see each other the way a man does, do they?
I decided Ben must know what you really wanted.'

'He didn't.' Clea's throat was dry. Ben hadn't even
come within a million miles of understanding her. He
had been too busy seeing her the way he wanted to see
her.

'To be frank, I talked this over with my guy. He said,
leave it alone, mind your own business.'

'Perceptive of him.'

'He isn't fond of Ben,' Natalie said, smiling.

'I can imagine why.'

'But I stopped caring about Ben that way years before I met Joe. And since I met Joe there hasn't been
any doubt about it. I mean, I really go for Joe. He's it,
if you know what I mean.'

Clea softened slightly, seeing the smile in the other girl's hard face. 'Yes, I know what you mean.'

'And I'd like Ben to have that feeling, too. He's an old friend. Although I'm not interested in him like that any more, I'm fond of him. He's worried me a lot sometimes. Haven't you ever noticed that it's people who have fixed ideas that come apart sooner or later? That's what you've done to Ben. He's fallen apart.'

Clea shifted her hands, her body weight moving with them. She stared at her own shoes. 'I appreciate what you're trying to do, but I just don't want to know.'

'I don't believe you,' said Natalie, and Clea looked up, her lips parted in surprise.

Natalie met her eyes, grimacing. 'You aren't indifferent to Ben. Don't pretend you are.'

'I didn't say I was indifferent,' Clea said angrily. 'I hate him!'

'Oh,' Natalie said on a long-drawn note of understanding. 'I get you.' She grinned.

Clea didn't like that grin. 'It isn't funny,' she said.

'I don't know,' Natalie murmured. 'Everything's funny from one angle or another.'

'To some people it may be.'

'Don't you think life's a bit of a joke?'

'I've never seen it like that,' she shrugged.

'Maybe that's why you've managed to bring Ben down. Although he pretends to laugh at everything in sight, I've always suspected that inside he's not seeing any joke either.'

Clea registered that, frowning.

'Ben's ... I suppose you'd say, intense,' Natalie said. 'He takes life seriously.'

'He takes himself seriously,' Clea said bitterly.

'Don't they all? Men are all the same.' Natalie looked at her with cynical amusement.

'No,' Clea denied, 'not all. That's the trouble with generalisations—they skate over the surface of everything. They may be a stab at a truth, but they often miss altogether.'

'God, listening to you is just like listening to Ben! You have more in common than you're prepared to admit.'

Clea felt tired. She didn't want to discuss Ben any longer. It made her eyes sting with hot tears to think about him.

'I must get back to work,' she said, straightening away from the desk. 'I'm sorry, there's nothing else I can say.'

'See Ben,' urged Natalie, standing between her and the door.

Clea shook her head.

'Don't you care that he's in such a state over you?' Natalie sounded irritable now, accusing. 'I'm not standing by and watching him eat his heart out.'

'Don't be absurd!' snapped Clea, side-stepping to reach the door. She opened it and Natalie swore, loudly enough to attract attention in the foyer, heads turning to stare at them.

Clea flushed. Janet, open-mouthed, was watching her as though dying to know what was going on between her and Natalie.

'Look,' Natalie said, moving to her side and lowering her voice. 'Look, how about meeting him on neutral ground? What harm can there be in that? Come to dinner with me and Joe and I'll get Ben along.'

'No,' Clea said stubbornly.

She walked away to the desk and after a moment Natalie went after her and slid through the gap in the counter. She looked at Clea across the polished wood.

'Think about it, anyway.'

Clea turned away without answering to pick up the phone. Natalie walked away, her head vibrant in the sunlight.

Next morning Clea answered the phone and Natalie said: 'Look, have you thought?'

Angrily, Clea snapped: 'Stop pestering me!'

'Come to dinner and I will.'

'Can't you understand English?'

'Ben's at the bottom of a big black well and I'm not leaving him there,' said Natalie in a rush of fierce words. 'Friends should do more than just pat you on the back and say: never mind. I've told Ben he should come and see you, hang around until you talk to him, but he just shakes his head and says you'll never forgive him. I don't know what he did to you, but he's only flesh and blood, you know, and you're hurting him badly.'

'Mind your own damned business!' snapped Clea, hanging up. But although Natalie didn't ring up again Clea was stuck with that little image of Ben at the bottom of a deep, black well. She knew the feeling. She had been down that well herself; in fact, she was still there. That thought made her feel odd. She and Ben were each at the bottom of deep black wells, separately and alone, and that seemed suddenly very silly.

'Life's too short,' Janet groaned as someone finally left after spending twenty minutes complaining about the quality of room service he had had at the hotel.

'Hasn't he got anything better to do with his time? I know I have.'

Life was too short, Clea thought, as she went out to lunch. Time was the enemy. It was a tide eating up the land of life, eroding it day by day, minute by minute. One day it would all have gone.

Ben had behaved unforgivably to her. She had told herself she would never forgive him and she had meant it at that moment. It already seemed a long time ago. That part of her life was buried deep under time's sea-green swell and could never be reclaimed. The future was still hers, though, and she was wasting it every second she refused to face the one inescapable fact about the situation.

She loved Ben, though she didn't want to. He had given her no cause to love him; on the contrary, he had given her every cause to hate him. But love doesn't demand a cause. It has its own reasoning, its own motivation.

She was walking along Regent Street slowly, staring into the huge plate glass windows of shops and offices, her mind absorbed in her thoughts. It wasn't for a while that it dawned on her that she was being followed. She caught glimpses of him in the windows, elongated dark shadows loping along at her heels, just far enough away for him to be barely recognisable, but close enough for her to know that it was him.

She crossed the road, darting like a minnow through the thick stream of traffic.

She didn't look round, but she knew Ben had followed. She walked right the way down to Piccadilly and turned into Leicester Square. Her faithful shadow came along.

She went into a paperback book shop on a corner

near the square. Ben lurked like a spy, his long body trying to look invisible. Clea took her time choosing a book she didn't want and knew she wouldn't read.

She walked back to the hotel with him at her heels like a lost dog, not coming up beside her but never being shaken off. Clea pretended not to have noticed him. He gave her the impression he was trying to look pathetic—but maybe it was just that he did look rather pathetic, his wide shoulders hunched in a defensive fashion, his black head tense as he weaved in and out behind her, keeping his eyes fixed on her at every step so that he several times almost knocked people down. She heard an old lady tut impatiently and Ben mumble with sheepish embarrassment, aware that she could hear the little altercation.

New tactics, she thought, going into the hotel. But how much of it was just tactics and how much was genuine?

Had Ben intended to speak to her? Or had he just wanted to see her? She had a very flushed face as she took over from Janet, who was having lunch at the hotel that day. They could eat in the staff dining-room, if they wished, but Clea preferred to get out of the hotel altogether for a short break. She spent enough hours there as it was.

Natalie rang up again next day. 'I won't be put off,' she threatened. 'I'll keep asking until you say yes.'

'Why don't you just mind your own business?' Clea asked wearily.

'If you saw an accident about to happen wouldn't you try to stop it? Well, Ben's an accident if ever I saw one.'

'If I see him once more——' Clea began, and Natalie burst out eagerly:

'Just once, that's all he wants, a chance to talk to you.'

'Why can't he take no for an answer?' Clea muttered.

'He has,' Natalie admitted. 'He's given up hope. But I hate to see him in such a low mood.'

'You really think a lot of him, don't you?' said Clea curiously.

'A hell of a lot,' Natalie admitted.

'I wouldn't have thought your Joe would like that much.'

'He knows how it is—I've told him. Ben's an old friend and I'd do a lot for him. He isn't any more than a friend, though. You don't know Ben well or you'd realise he's quite à guy.'

Clea sighed. 'I know him well enough.' Too well. Much too well, she thought grimly.

'I liked Ben the way he was before he met you,' Natalie said with a faint hostility. 'He was full of life. You've run over him like a steamroller.'

'He deserved it.'

Natalie groaned. 'What harm can there be in a little dinner for four? I swear to you Joe and I will be there. Word of honour, this time no tricks.'

Clea hesitated, and Natalie pressed the advantage she could sense she had pained. 'Please!'

'Oh, all right,' Clea sighed with a sensation of sheer weariness. She believed Natalie. The other girl would go on and on until she gave in to her demand.

'When's your next free evening?'

Clea told her and was given Natalie's address. 'Eight o'clock?' Natalie asked, and Clea agreed. She knew she was going to regret this, but now that she had said yes she couldn't back out again.

The weather broke next morning. Rain poured down

as though someone up in the sky was chucking it at London. The gutters ran with it. The windows streamed all day and people took on a harassed look as they ducked in and out of the hotel.

Clea took time during her lunch-break to buy herself a new dress. The clothes she had brought with her from Greece weren't warm enough now that the Indian summer was over. She chose a soft blue wool dress with a tight smooth bodice and pleated skirt which swirled when she moved, showing a good deal of her long legs.

She wore it on the evening she was to have dinner with Natalie and the two men. She had to take a taxi to Natalie's flat because she did not know how to find it. Natalie opened the door and gave her a delighted grin.

'Oh, you came—thanks!'

Clea walked past her as she waved her forward and Natalie went on talking: 'I'm not certain Ben will actually come. He isn't going out much these days. I had a hunch you might not turn up and I didn't want to raise his hopes in case you didn't, so I didn't tell him.'

Clea stopped in the act of taking off her new winter coat. 'What? He doesn't know I'm coming?'

'It will be a surprise,' Natalie explained.

'You seem fond of them,' Clea muttered bitterly.

Natalie looked taken aback and grimaced. 'Oh sorry about that. I did think I was playing Cupid, you know, bringing two star-crossed lovers together.'

'Well, put your bow and arrows away,' Clea said crossly, and someone behind her laughed.

She looked round. 'This is Joe,' said Natalie, going to link her arm through his and smiling.

'Hi,' he said, offering Clea a hand. 'So you're the cause of Ben's downfall. I'm glad to meet you.'

He was tall and thin, his fair hair curly and rough, his eyes pale blue and very observant. Clea felt them inspecting her as they shook hands.

'Come and have a drink,' Joe suggested. 'What will you have?' He led the way into the tiny sitting-room and Clea sat down beside Natalie on the leather couch.

'Sherry,' she accepted. 'Thanks.'

'Sweet?'

'Please.'

Natalie was looking at her dress. 'That's nice. How are you finding the weather? It must be different from Greece.'

'Of course it's different from Greece,' Joe teased. 'Don't complain about English weather, though. We've had a great autumn so far.'

'So far,' Natalie said drily, cocking her head. They all listened to the running sound of rain down the windows.

The door bell went and Clea tensed, her hand shaking so that some of her sherry spilled and she could busy herself with rubbing a handkerchief over her skirt. Natalie got up and went out.

'Now the balloon goes up,' Joe said drily.

Natalie was talking fast and nervously. 'You're soaking! How did you get that wet?'

'In case you hadn't noticed, it's raining,' Ben answered, his deep cool voice making Clea's nerves leap with fire.

'What were you doing? Swimming in it? This coat is saturated! Don't you own an umbrella?'

'Don't fuss,' said Ben, walking into the sitting-room.

He stopped dead, his face whitening, and Clea looked
at him, very flushed. His black hair was clinging to his
skull, shining with rain, his skin had a glistening damp-
ness which emphasised the tight shock which was clamp-
ing his teeth together.

'What the hell . . .' he began.

'Clea's having dinner with us,' Natalie said brightly.

'This was your idea!' Ben accused, turning on her
with cold furious eyes. 'I thought I told you to mind
your own business?'

'Drink, Ben?' Joe was at the sideboard, a glass in
his hand. Ben ignored him, turning back to Clea.

'How did she get you here? Another of her little
tricks, I suppose. I'm sorry, I wasn't in on it this time—
I swear I wasn't.'

'I know you weren't,' Clea murmured.

Joe and Natalie slid out of the room and neither
of the two left in it noticed. The door closed quietly.
Clea looked up at the tiny sound and her eyes met
Ben's. He had been watching her with a hungry intensity, his mouth a straight line.

'You look very lovely,' he said deeply.

'Thank you.' She smoothed down one of the pleats
in her skirt, her hand trembling a little.

Ben's gaze fixed on the little movement. He drew
an unsteady breath and then he was on his knees beside her, his black head bent to touch his mouth to
her hand. 'Oh, Clea, Clea!'

She didn't pull her hand away, but watched him,
her heart beating so fast it drowned every other sound
in the room. Slowly she put her other hand up to
brush back the damp hair from his forehead.

'Don't hate me, Clea,' Ben whispered huskily. 'I

know I deserve it, but don't. You put me though weeks of misery. I've paid for what I did to you. Must I go on paying for the rest of my life? I love you. I think I'd die if I knew for certain I was never going to hold you in my arms again.'

She saw a tiny pulse beating in the side of his throat. She watched it, counting the beats, matching her own heartbeat with them, her whole mind drowned in the agony and happiness of being with him.

'Aren't you going to say anything to me?' He was kissing her palm, her fingers, slowly, his mouth warm and not very steady. 'Say something, Clea—anything! I want to hear your voice.'

She couldn't think of anything to say except his name, so she said that in a husky whisper, and the next moment Ben was holding her in his arms, his mouth searching blindly for hers.

Clea yielded, her arms round his neck, as desperate to accept his kiss as he was to give it. The intensity of feeling to which she surrendered beat between them like a flame and when at last Ben lifted his head, her eyes were drowsy with the after-effect of a passion which had left her trembling.

'Oh, God,' Ben muttered thickly. 'Do you know how much I've needed that? I can't begin to tell you.'

Beneath his urgency she could see that elation she had seen once before, but this time it did not make her hate him. Ben could have his moment of triumph. She looked at him with the smiling indulgence of a woman who knows she is loved.

He closed his eyes, his mouth wry. 'Do you know, at first I was convinced you'd come back to me? I wouldn't admit to myself that you'd walked out for good. I was so sure of you. For days I drove around London like a lunatic, looking for you, haunting every restaurant, every pub, in the hope of seeing you. I wore down gradually, bit by bit, to the point of admitting you'd really gone and didn't mean to come back. That was the lowest point of my life.'

'Did it hurt?' Clea wanted to hear him admit it had. He had hurt her so badly. She needed to know she wasn't the only one who had suffered.

'Like hell,' he grimaced. 'I made myself unpopular with all my friends. They thought I was going off my rocker. I was a man possessed. I looked for you all the time, everywhere I went.'

'Natalie did say you were behaving like a lunatic.'

He laughed, his hard face wry. 'That's an understatement! I'd been so confident, so certain of you. I thought all I had to do was get you into bed once and that would be that.'

'I remember,' Clea said with faint acidity.

'Yes,' said Ben, looking at her with unusual humility. 'I was a swine.'

'You were.'

He stroked her hair, his hand trembling. 'Forgive me, darling. It served me right, crashing to my knees like that. I was talking about love when all the time I just meant sex—you were right about that. I didn't admit to myself I really loved you until I thought it was too late.'

'Not too late, Ben,' she said huskily.

He picked up her hand and kissed it. 'You'll marry me? I don't think I could bear to let you out of my sight again in case you disappear.'

'Yes,' she said, and he kissed her again, his mouth

demanding. A little tap at the door made them start. Ben growled under his breath, then said: 'Oh, come in, Natalie.'

She peered round the door, viewing them both with approval as she took in their entwined bodies. 'All signed, sealed and delivered?'

'I ought to wring your neck,' said Ben, his eyes laughing a mock-threat. 'You interfering little darling!'

Much flattered, she grinned back at him. 'Don't mention it—just leave a tip when you go. Are you two beyond such mundane matters as food or can we have dinner now?'

Ben looked at Clea, smiling. 'Hungry?'

'Starving,' she admitted.

'Even lovers have to eat,' Natalie teased.

Ben stood up, pulling Clea with him, his hand round her wrist in a possessive clasp. 'We'll be with you in one minute, Natalie.'

She gave them a wry look. 'I'll keep the soup hot, but keep it short, will you? Joe and I are ravenous!'

When the door had closed again Ben kissed Clea's nose. 'I just want to say one thing before we join them.'

'Yes?' She traced the strong line of forehead, cheek and jaw with contented eyes.

'I love you,' Ben whispered, and then he started to kiss her all over again.

The Mills & Boon Rose is the Rose of Romance

Every month there are ten new titles to choose from — ten new stories about people falling in love, people you want to read about, people in exciting, far-away places. Choose Mills & Boon. It's your way of relaxing:

February's titles are:

TEMPLE OF FIRE by *Margaret Way*
Julian Stanford had everything except a heart. Could Fleur possibly stand up to him and his overwhelming family?

ONE BRIEF SWEET HOUR by *Jane Arbor*
If Dale Ransome still chose to think the worst of Lauren, let him. She just didn't care any more — did she?

WHEN MAY FOLLOWS by *Betty Neels*
Had Katrina been incredibly foolish to want to change her life by marrying Professor Raf van Tellerinck?

LIVING TOGETHER by *Carole Mortimer*
The attractive Leon Masters was determined to get through the ice that enclosed Helen — but was his method the right one?

SEDUCTION by *Charlotte Lamb*
Clea wasn't too enthusiastic about her arranged marriage to Ben Winter, until he came along to turn her feelings upside down . . .

A GIRL POSSESSED by *Violet Winspear*
Was Janie a good enough actress to conceal her love for Pagan Pentrevah, and pretend to be married to him to keep his ex-wife at bay?

THE SUGAR DRAGON by *Victoria Gordon*
The forceful Con Bradley was quite enough for Verna to cope with, even before Madeline Cunningham arrived, with wedding bells in mind!

NEVER COUNT TOMORROW by *Daphne Clair*
Lin fell in love with Soren Wingard and everything crashed about her in ruins. Could she get away from him before she did any more harm?

ICEBERG by *Robyn Donald*
What heart Justin Doyle had belonged to his dead wife Alison. Hadn't Linnet better leave Justin to her sister Bronwyn?

AN ISLAND LOVING by *Jan MacLean*
All Kristin knew was that he brought her more happiness — and bitter unhappiness — than she had ever known. Would she ever be free of him again?

If you have difficulty in obtaining any of these books from your local paperback retailer, write to:

Mills & Boon Reader Service
P.O. Box 236, Thornton Road, Croydon, Surrey, CR9 3RU.

The Mills & Boon Rose is the Rose of Romance

GREGG BARRATT'S WOMAN by *Lilian Peake*
Why was that disagreeable Gregg Barratt so sure that what had happened to Cassandra was her sister Tanis's fault?

FLOODTIDE by *Kay Thorpe*
A stormy relationship rapidly grew between Dale Ryland and Jos Blakeman. What had Jos to give anyone but bitterness and distrust?

SAY HELLO TO YESTERDAY by *Sally Wentworth*
It had to be coincidence that Holly's husband Nick — whom she had not seen for seven years — was on this remote Greek island? Or was it?

BEYOND CONTROL by *Flora Kidd*
Kate was in love with her husband Sean Kierly, but what was the point of clinging to a man who so obviously didn't love her?

RETRIBUTION by *Charlotte Lamb*
Why had the sophisticated Simon Hilliard transferred his attentions from Laura's sister to Laura herself, who wasn't as capable as her sister of looking after herself?

A SECRET SORROW by *Karen van der Zee*
Could Faye Sherwood be sure that Kai Ellington's love would stand the test if and when she told him her tragic secret?

MASTER OF MAHIA by *Gloria Bevan*
Lee's problem was to get away from New Zealand and the dour Drew Hamilton. Or *was* that her real problem?

TUG OF WAR by *Sue Peters*
To Dee Lawrence's dismay and fury every time she met Nat Archer, he always got the better of her. Why didn't he just go away?

CAPTIVITY by *Margaret Pargeter*
Chase Marshall had offered marriage to Alex, simply because he thought she was suitable. Well, he could keep his offer!

TORMENTED LOVE by *Margaret Mayo*
Amie's uncle had hoped she would marry his heir Oliver Maxwell. But how could she marry a maddening man like that?

If you have difficulty in obtaining any of these books from your local paperback retailer, write to:

Mills & Boon Reader Service
P.O. Box 236, Thornton Road, Croydon, Surrey, CR9 3RU.
Available March 1981

Masquerade
Historical Romances

Intrigue
excitement
romance

LADY OF STARLIGHT
by Margot Holland

Gilbert de Boveney saved Lady Alyce de Beaumont
from the lust of a neighbouring Count, but it was his
twin brother she longed to marry. Or was it?

CAMILLA
by Sara Orwig

Camilla Hyde's only hope of escaping from the British
troops devastating Washington in 1814 lay with Jared
Kingston. He had made it clear that he was not
interested in her, but she would have travelled with the
Devil himself to get home to England!

Look out for these titles in your local paperback shop from
13th February 1981